For those who struggle with dyslexia

and

my parents and grandparents

The Near Extinction of Dragons

A NOVEL BY

L.F. EHRL

Contents

The Near Extinction of Dragons

CHAPTER 1

Lost and Found

I AWOKE STARTLED AS IF having a bad dream I could not remember. My heart was pounding hard and fast in my chest to the point I could feel it in my throat. I was under a large old willow tree. The thick hanging green branches enclosed me, keeping me hidden from the outside world. My long raven black hair was tangled and knotted from blowing in the wind. A long vine was wrapped around my ankles. My head was throbbing in pain as I tried to ignore it and focus on unwrapping the vine from my legs. Once the vine was unwrapped, I stood on the soft green grass that was under my feet tickling my toes. I was wearing a long white dress stained with dirt and grime down to my kneecaps. It was tattered and ripped at the bottom, and its sleeves looked like they were torn off.

The morning sun was rising over the uneven horizon, leaving behind a warm glowing orange sky. The cold clear morning air had left me with a handful of questions and not a single answer. *Who am I? Where am I, and what do I do now?* Something was moving in the tall grass and heading straight toward me. As it got closer, I saw it was a black cat. The cat had different colored eyes: one was dark forest green, and the other was light sky blue. It had a tear on its left ear and was giving me a curious look. Yet it looked so familiar as if I had seen this particular cat before.

"Hey, do you know where I am?" I asked the cat.

The cat then stretched its long thin body and started moving very quickly away from me.

"Where are you going?" I asked, chasing after him.

He was heading west, away from the orange sunrise, which was slowly turning into a soft yellow glow. The cat had no problem making its way through the thick, overgrown forest. I followed the cat as best as I could while tripping and stumbling over the uneven forest ground. A few times, I thought I had lost the cat, but then it seemed to be waiting for me to catch up, and once I did, the cat scurried ahead. As I made my way over a large tree that was lying on the forest floor, the cat seemed to have vanished into thin air. I fell to the ground feeling tired, hungry, lost, scared, and confused. My heart was pounding, my head still hurt, and once again I thought, *Who am I? Where am I, and what do I do next?* I had given up all hope and lay on the cold damp forest floor.

Then I heard movement behind me, and an old raspy voice said, "Hello."

I jumped up and turned around, and I saw an old woman. The old woman was wearing an old brown dress that was tattered, torn, and stained. Her long gray hair was down, hanging past the middle of her back. Her hair was disheveled, and there were leaves and a small stick in it.

"Hi," I said, as I jumped up.

"Are you ok?" asked the old woman. "There is dried blood on your forehead."

My eyes widened. I reached up and touched my forehead and immediately winced in pain, instantly regretting my decision to touch my forehead.

"What is your name?" the old woman asked, with a curious look on her face.

"I don't know who I am or where I am."

The old lady studied me for a moment and then smiled. She said her name was Nessa. She said she was the healer for the village of Arm. She seemed clever but weak owing to her old age. She told me she was in the woods collecting herbs for medicine. After looking at my head wound, she said, "You'll live. You can help me collect some herbs for my medicine, and I can put an antibiotic ointment made with oregano, ginger, garlic, and honey on your wound."

"Sure," I said, without a moment of hesitation. "Arm—that is an interesting name." I tried my best not to sound rude, but I was trying to get some sense of where I was.

Unfortunately, Nessa said that it was a perfect fit for this place. She gave me a list of things to collect. Her handwriting was small and very detailed. On the list were herbs and what they were used for: oregano for antibacterial, low energy, depression, and headaches; lavender for muscle spasms; marjoram for ear pain, headaches, and anxiety; garlic for skin infections and for a cold or flu, along with many more herbs and plants. When we were picking herbs, I decided to try to get some more answers, but Nessa was too focused on collecting to make any kind of conversation.

In a shady area, there looked to be a bush of snowy white flowers that were tulip shaped and had dull green leaves. It was a beautiful flower, so I went to pick one. Nessa noticed me walking over to the bush and pulled me away from it by my arm.

Nessa said, "Don't pick those, my dear. Those are Moon Lilies, also known as The Bloom of the Sacred Datura. Every part of them is poisonous, even its sap and seeds. Moon Lilies used to be used for medicine before they were found to be poisonous."

When we finished, we walked into the town. Nessa asked everyone whom we met if they had ever seen me before, but no one knew who I was or where I was from. The town of Arm was very small with poorly constructed old buildings that were in dire need of repair. They looked as if a single strong wind would cause them to crash to the ground, breaking into hundreds of pieces. I asked her why the town was in such a bad shape.

"There is a Minotaur village on the opposite side of the island, and it is fairly big, taking up more than half of the island. Sometimes, someone from the village trespasses or tries to steal their crops because our soil has too much clay and sand in it to grow anything. They come here and destroy our village in retaliation."

I was shocked and asked, "Why doesn't anyone help you?"

"The person in charge of our village is Theron. He hates humans. There was a retired nomad who often gave us fruits and vegetables. Unfortunately, very recently, her house burnt down to the ground in a fire with her inside it."

I wanted to ask what she meant by not liking humans, but the look on her face told me I would only regret it. While walking around on the uneven dirt and dust roads, I noticed everyone I passed gave me suspicious looks with a hollowness in their doll-like eyes, which I found unsettling.

At sunset, we headed to Nessa's home. It was a small cottage on the outskirts of the town, and it had one single lantern light on inside. She walked in the door where there was a one-armed man who looked like he had gotten into a bad fight. His clothes were dirty and oversized. He had very greasy hair, and he smelled like he had never bathed in his life.

He then said, "That will be two gold pieces for watching your thing."

"That's expensive, don't you think? And that thing is a sweet baby girl," Nessa said irritably.

The man said, "You were gone a long time, so now it's two golden pieces. If you don't like it, I can always raise the price even more."

Nessa sighed and gave him two gold coins that had a dragon on one side and a crown on the other. Before the man left, Nessa said, "Why don't you buy some manners with that money?"

The man did not reply but gave Nessa an irritated scowl, then he went on his way. The cottage was small with six cots all side by side, a wooden desk, and a fireplace with a cauldron. The smell of the food cooking in the cauldron reminded me that I had not yet eaten today. Nessa took out two wooden bowls and a loaf of bread, and we sat in silence and ate what appeared to be some type of soup. I am not sure I had ever tasted anything like it before. It wasn't bad, just different. Its flavor was overwhelming with spices and herbs. I was grateful she shared her food with me. Then I heard crying. I looked up and saw Nessa holding a baby no older than a few days wrapped in a tan ripped swaddle.

"What is her name?" I asked.

"I don't know. I haven't picked one yet," Nessa said, frowning, and said the baby's mother had died in labor. "I tried my best to save her, but I couldn't stop the bleeding. My son, her father, was a soldier who lost his life, so now I'm all she has."

"Ms. Nessa, can you tell me more about where I am?"

Nessa rocked the baby in her arms trying to shush her, and she explained to me that we were on the island of Arm. "Arm has a small crowded village. It is the smallest, poorest, and most brutal in this world of ours that holds some real evil. You must be careful, Angel. I have decided I am going to call you Angel." She continued, "People here are starving. People here go missing, and there are rumors that these missing people are ending up on the dinner menu. So be careful of your surroundings, and never enter a building where you are not 100 percent sure that you are safe. Some people will try to trick you, but you must never let your guard down. This is the cruel world we live in."

"If this place is so bad Ms. Nessa, why don't you leave?"

Nessa said, "I grew up here. My mother was a healer. I have thought about leaving, but there are good people here who count on me and my healing medicines. As long as there are good people here, I have decided I'll stay, and when they leave, so will I. The evil people of Arm do not bother with me. There were rumors years ago that I was a witch, so I let them believe that. So what are you really doing here? And don't call me Ms. Nessa; just plain Nessa is fine." Nessa was now glaring at me.

I told her how I had awoken in the forest under an old willow tree, how I had followed a black cat for hours until I lost it and, not long after, she had found me on the ground, hungry, tired, and lost. I again told her that I didn't know who I was or where I came from and that I was not sure what I was supposed to do now. Nessa studied me for a moment, then smiled and nodded, and then said that, if I helped her, she would help me figure out who I was.

She placed her hand on mine and said, "Do not worry, my dear; we will figure this out together. You can stay here as long as you like, and I can use your help making and selling my healing medicines."

When she put her hand on mine, I noticed an old slightly dented gold ring. I looked at her questionably and asked, "Are you married?"

She looked down at her ring and hesitated for a moment before responding, "Yes. At one time I was married. My husband has long since passed, unfortunately." She was now fiddling with the ring still on her finger.

"What was he like?"

She smiled and replied, "He was a lot less stubborn than I am. He was my rock just as much as I was his. He could always make the room smile and laugh, even in the most heartbreaking of situations. We never had much, but if I am being honest, I would rather have a single rose given to me by him than a chest full of jewelry and gold given to me by any other man. Now that's enough small talk. These old bones of mine are ready for bed, but before we head off to bed, let me put some of my herbs on that cut on your head."

Nessa applied her antibiotic ointment made of oregano, ginger, garlic, and honey. She then gave me white willow bark, ginger, and turmeric tea. The tea had a strong, unusual smell. I did not argue with her since I was tired. I drank it quickly, and we both headed to bed.

The next day, Nessa had me deliver medicine to some of the villagers to help earn my keep for staying with her. She told me to only charge them one gold piece per medicine if they were able to pay.

Before I left, she stopped me and said, "No matter what you do, only go to the addresses on the list."

I told her that I understood and that I would not go to any other address.

"If you go into a place that's not on this list, you won't ever come out—well, not in one piece anyway."

I had understood from our talk the night before how danger-ous the village of Arm was. A lot of families in Arm shared the same house. Many were multi-generational, but there were also families who chose to live together because they lacked finances and also had safety concerns. At the end of the day, of the sixteen bottles I had delivered, I had collected only six gold coins. I had the sack of coins tied around my waist with a rope like a belt. I wore an old sweater that Nessa had given me to conceal the small bag of coins. People continued to stare at me on the street. Some people stopped in their tracks to whisper and point at me. No one said hello or gave a friendly smile or waved. Some people were missing limbs; others had scars or open cuts and fresh bruises. Everyone was extremely thin as if they hadn't eaten in weeks.

I had just dropped off the last of the medicine when a young boy came running toward me. When he was in front of me, he fell to his knees. His eyes were red and puffy, and as he cried, a river of snot ran down his face.

He spoke in a shaking voice, "Ms. help please. My mother has fainted, and she is not moving. Please, I beg of you to help her. Help her please." His face was buried in the bottom of my dress, but I could hear him clearly as he spoke loudly.

I said calmly to the boy, "Ok, show me where your mother fainted."

"Thank you.; thank you. She fainted at home. Follow me."

I nodded, and he took off running with me right behind him. The house he stopped at was nicer than some of the others. It was made of large stones with a straw-thatched roof and a large sturdy old door. It was so well made that even the faintest light could get inside it. It looked more stable than the other houses on either side of it. He ran in with no hesitation, and I followed.

The second I ran into the house, the door slammed shut behind me. There was very little light, only a single small lantern. The first thing I noticed was that there was no woman collapsed on the ground. There was a thin man with long blonde hair and an extra-large nose with red growths all over it. That made him look extremely ugly.

"Nice job, kid," said the ugly man. He then turned his attention to me and said, "Now hand over everything you got, and we'll consider sparing your life."

Another man then stepped out of the shadows and stood in front of the door. I scanned the room looking for another exit and saw that the boy, the two men, and I were the only ones in the room. The second man was fairly muscular, bald with not the slightest bit of hair, and covered in all sorts of scars, like he had been in multiple fights and lost. My mind was going a million miles a minute. They had lured me into this house to rob me and who knows what else. There were two small windows, but they were so small that even a child couldn't escape through them. The house was about the size of Nessa's small house, maybe a little bigger. The bald man with scars was blocking the only door, so I could not escape. The boy was silently watching.

The blonde man ran at me with a cleaver held tightly in his hand. He swiped at me, but I dodged and caught his wrist with the cleaver and snapped it fairly easily, causing it to fall from his grasp. His wrist was now limp as he howled in pain. I then punched him in the jaw and threw him into the boy, causing them both to go flying into the wall. The boy's head was one of the first things that made contact with the wall causing him to fall unconscious. The thin ugly blonde man tried to cushion the fall with his leg but failed horribly, causing him more pain as he curled up in a ball holding his leg and screaming.

The bald man with the scars stepped in front of me and said, "Now you've done it, you vile wench."

He grabbed my arm, and when he did, I punched him in the rib cage and heard a loud, sharp cracking sound, like the breaking of one or two of his ribs. He whimpered in pain and then loosened his grip slightly on my arm. I took advantage at that moment and grabbed him by the throat. I threw him to the door as hard as I possibly could. He went flying, hitting the door so hard that he bent the frame and the door flew open. The bald man's jaw was not the slightest bit lined up the way it should be. He was now curled up in a ball on the ground, crying quietly and moaning.

He looked at me in shock and fearfully said, "What are you? Are you a she-devil from hell?"

I ran out through the open door and into the busy dirt road, trying to absorb what had just happened. People came from all around to find out what all the commotion was coming from the little stone house. I panicked and started running, not knowing how the people would react to me after taking down two grown men and a child. While running, it finally hit me what I had just done. I had beaten up two fully grown adults who had weapons and I barely had a scratch. I wondered how I did that. How am I so strong, and where did I learn to fight?

It was sunset when I returned to Nessa's cottage. There was a black cat sitting on the front step. He looked like the cat I had followed through the woods the day before. He even had the same tear in his left ear. He was stretched out as if he had nothing better to do. At that moment, a sense of familiarity rushed over me, and it was strangely calming.

I bent down to stroke his soft black fur, but when I was about to pet him, I heard Nessa asking, "Who's there?"

"It's me," I called back.

I turned back to the cat, but he was now gone. I shook my head, thinking my mind was playing tricks on me, and headed inside. I saw Nessa holding the baby as she fed her a bottle of goat's milk. The bag of coins was still tied around my waist. I untied the bag from my waist and dropped the bag of coins next to her on the cot before I laid down on a cot nearby.

Nessa turned to me and said, "Angel, how was your day in town today?"

I hesitated, then said, "A young boy came up to me and said—"

But before I could finish, Nessa cut in and said, "The boy needed your help, and a family member was endangered or sick."

I was shocked and replied, "Yes. How did you know?"

She shook her head. "They are getting smarter at luring people. I'll give them that. How did you escape?"

I was about to reply when there was a booming knock at the door. The knock was so loud that it startled all of us, even the baby, causing her to wake up crying. I sat up. Nessa handed the baby to me to try and soothe her and answered the door. It was the blonde man, the bald man with the scars, and the young boy. The blonde man's face was swollen from the injuries to his jaw. His right wrist hung limply from where it had snapped earlier that day. The bald man with the scars was holding his ribs but had a black and blue bruise on his forehead above his right eye. He was always ugly but was now even uglier with his face so swollen that he could barely open his eyes. The boy who was being carried had his arm around the bald man's neck. He was probably hurt when I threw the blonde man at him.

The bald man with the scars said to Nessa, "Woman, we need medical attention quickly because we were attacked by a group of thieves."

Before he could finish, the blonde man and boy spotted me and slowly started to back away.

The bald man with the scars noticed their movement and asked, "What are you doing?"

They both pointed in my direction. The bald man's eyes opened so wide I thought they were going to pop out of his head. In less than a second, they all scrambled, hobbling down the path, at times tripping over their own feet trying to get away from me.

Nessa turned to me and said, "Did you do that to those men, my angel?" I nodded, not looking her in the eyes. She said, "Look at me."

When I did, I saw she had a big smile on her face. Nessa said, "You can stay as long as you like, and honestly, they deserved what you did to them."

I asked Nessa, "Did they ever try to do that to you?"

She came next to me and held my hand. "Honestly, no, but I am the only healer left in Arm, so they know that, if they tried to pull that with me, I would never treat them with any of my medicines ever again. Now come along. We need our rest."

We ate some of the leftover soup and then headed to bed.

That night and the day following, the image of the men and the boy and the events of the stone house, and all the possibilities that could have happened, ran continuously through my mind. If I had just missed one of the punches I threw, or if they had landed one of theirs, it could have been a very different outcome for me. The blonde man could have cut me to pieces with the cleaver. The bald man could have grabbed my face and crushed it in a couple of seconds. The boy could have tripped me and helped hold me down as the other two robbed me and hurt me.

I continued to give out medicine for Nessa for the next few days. Now everyone in town—well, almost everyone—was terrified of me, and I am grateful. I am now walking a little taller, and now I carry a small knife in my pocket. I am not looking for trouble, but knowing I can defend myself is giving me more self-confidence.

A few nights later, in the middle of the night, we were all woken up by crashing and screaming. Nessa grabbed the baby and told me we needed to go into the forest and hide. We ran out of the cottage and saw that there was a raid. We watched in horror as a man was struck down right in front of us and his blood splattered on us. The creature had two long twisted horns on its head, and his body was muscular. He had the head of a bull, sharp teeth, and large eyes. It had two muscular arms with talons instead of hands or fingers. It had strong thick legs and a long tail. The creature was over eight feet tall and wore armor over his chest with an armor-type kilt. The creature was a Minotaur.

I picked up the eight-inch knife the dead man had dropped in front of me and hid behind a tree. The Minotaur walked away without noticing I was there. I jumped on its back and slit its throat. Hot red bubbling blood fell from the cut and onto my hand, so hot that it immediately burnt the skin on my hand. I struggled to hold back a scream from the pain. My skin instantly bubbled with blisters. I jumped off its back as it fell forward, and that's where its dead body lay. I took down two more Minotaurs before the knife broke because of their strong ash skin.

I heard crying. Nessa was running back to her cabin, which was ablaze.

I ran after her and called out, "Nessa, there is nothing we can do for the house now."

I took the baby, grabbed Nessa's hand, and ran. We moved deep into the forest until we felt safe. We stayed there for hours, not saying a word out of fear of being heard. Luckily, the baby was quiet and slept, never making a sound. Hours later, the sun rose, and we headed back to Arm. The Minotaurs preferred darkness and normally headed back to their village before sunrise. Less than half of the town's people had survived, including Nessa, the baby, and I.

There was nothing left; everything was burned to the ground. The bodies of villagers of Arm were everywhere. I looked around for a moment at all of them before starting to dig graves for the dead. These people had suffered a lifetime and had nothing; the least I could do for them was give them a proper burial. Nessa tended to the wounded. After hours of digging, all the bodies were buried, and we laid colorful wildflowers over the graves. We stayed there for a while until I felt a hand on my shoulder. I turned my head and saw Nessa shaking her head. I tried to comfort her, but it didn't work, so she turned away trying to hide her face. I could tell she was trying her best to hold back tears, then I looked back at the graves and saw the black cat was there. He looked ragged because of the scene he had just witnessed. The horror. . . No one from Arm could fathom the mass human genocide. It made me sick to my stomach.

I turned to see Nessa walking away.

"Kat," I said.

Nessa stopped, turned, and said, "Pardon?"

"Kat," I replied. "I think we should name the baby Kat."

Nessa said nothing, just stood there and nodded. We searched the ashes of Nessa's home to find anything useful. We found some coins, two rats running in the ashes, and a metal staff. The metal staff was about six feet tall. It was thicker at the top and had ridges that were worn away from being held by the previous owner. There were no other marking or identifying features.

I stopped and asked, "Why is there a metal staff?"

Nessa shrugged and said, "I don't ever remember seeing that before."

I was about to ask if maybe it had belonged to her husband.

"It belongs to you now," she said, so I just left it at that.

That night, I built a fire. Nessa found an aloe vera plant and removed some of its leaves and squeezed them until the aloe came out and then rubbed it on the burn on my hand from the Minotaur blood. That night we slept under the stars.

CHAPTER 2

A New Home

THE NEXT MORNING, WE HEADED to the dock and used the coins we had found to purchase three tickets on a ship heading to Bateau. We would be traveling across the Maris Sea, and with any luck, our voyage would take no longer than a week. We would have to share a small cabin with crew members who were assigned to night duty, so during the day, we would have to stay on deck to allow them to sleep.

Nessa said, "It is a beautiful day. Not a cloud in the sky."

I stood at the end of the dock, metal staff in hand, looking at the crystal-clear waters, trying to get a glimpse of what lay ahead of us. Around noon, the ship set sail. The large wooden ship, once dark wood, was faded and worn smooth. The sails were a patchwork of white; they had been pieced together from old sails that had long since seen better days. The haul had more than just a few scratches on it and was covered in spots with barnacles. The crew acted as if we were invisible.

"They might be great at catching fish, but they know nothing about catching a woman's heart or hospitality." When Nessa said that, all the crew in earshot gave her a dirty look.

During the day, I often helped the crew around the ship, and they taught me how to tie the seven essential knots: the bowline, figure eight, rolling hitch, square knot, reef knot, stopper knot, and lashing knots. Also, I learned how to steer the ship. My new routine was to get up before dawn and help out around the ship while Nessa took care of Kat. On the fourth day, the wind howled like wolves during a full moon and lightning flashed in the sky. The boat was smashing against the waves, bobbing up and down in the water so hard that I could barely stay standing. I overheard one crew member say to another that the wind was very Bora today, referring to the blowing of the strong cold wind.

Then I heard a loud crash. The ship was taking on water. There was a large hole on the starboard side. I ran below and grabbed my metal staff. Nessa was sitting, holding Kat tightly to her chest, and I directed her and Kat to a lifeboat. Some of the crew were already in a lifeboat; others were in line waiting to get aboard. Then a sea serpent emerged out of the water. It was dark blue, almost black, and had a large fin on its back with six horns on its head almost like a crown, and black dead eyes. I tightened my grip on my metal staff, ready to fight, to try and give the others time to escape. I jumped in the air, hitting it on the side of the head, then landed back on the sinking ship, but it wasn't very effective. The second time, I jumped and hit the sea monster. I still had no success in stopping it from advancing on the lifeboats. When I was in the air, it hit me with its tail, sending me into the ship on my back, knocking the air out of my lungs.

I watched as the beast was headed toward the passengers and crew who were trying to escape. They were all in lifeboats and were being lowered into the raging sea below. I knew I had to keep this beast busy so the others could get away. I stood taking what I thought could be my last breath. I jumped in the air feeling the rain pelting me. The beast was getting ready to strike, and that was when it happened. For a moment, time felt like it was standing still. The end of my staff now had a giant scythe. I swung the scythe with all the strength I had, and it was no longer as heavy as it had been. The beast's screams filled the air. I sliced through the right side of its face, leaving a large wound that cut off a piece of its upper jaw and part of its snout. The beast slithered back into the water and swam off in the opposite direction of the lifeboats.

The ship was now sinking faster. I threw myself into the water and I sank, unable to let go of the scythe still in my hand. Some of the crew who were waiting for me reached down deep in the water and managed to pull me in the lifeboat.

Once I was in the boat, one of the crew asked me, "What is your name again?"

I hesitated before replying, "Bora. My name is Bora."

Nessa smiled at me and said, "Bora suits you, my dear."

I nodded. The scythe was still in my hand, but it had turned back into the staff.

We stayed on the lifeboat for a few more days, surviving off fish and, with the help of a small goat Kat had, plenty of fresh milk.

Finally, we arrived at Bateau, a large village known for its expansive trade route, where you could buy fresh food and fishing supplies, boats, and foreign goods. The streets were always busy and loud as if they did not know the meaning of silence. As far as the eye could see, vendors lined street after street who were selling their overpriced products. The smell of the sea lingered heavily in the thick sodden air. You could almost taste the salt and the pungent fish with each breath. Bateau was one of the largest territories surrounded by water on one side, and its beaches stretched for miles. The weather was hot and humid, and it rained every day this time of year. The city of Bateau was old but was clean and well kept, and people came from hundreds of miles around to buy, sell, and trade. If you needed something, no matter how questionable it was, you could get it here.

There were posters everywhere with rankings of the hierarchy—King of Dragons, Dragons/Dragonesses, Therianthropy, Witch/Wizard, Assassins, and the lowest, Humans.

As I was reading a poster, I turned to Nessa and asked, "Who is the dragon king?

"That would be King Maverick who rules over our realm of Inue," she said.

"What Is Therianthropy?" I asked.

"Therianthropy is the ability to shapeshift into an animal form," Nessa said.

I then asked, "Do you know anyone who is a therianthropy?"

Nessa shook her head and said, "Not one, and I have never met anyone who has actually met one."

"Why are the posters here?"

She replied, "To remind us that we are on the bottom and that we are expendable after what our ancestors did."

I was about to ask her what she meant, when she said, in a harsh whisper, "Don't let anyone know we are from Arm."

I asked her why, and she said, "People will look down on us and we will have a harder time with lodging and job opportunities. Arm is where the poorest and worst of the worst are from. Saying you're from Arm is detrimental to your future."

I didn't know what to say, so I asked, "What do we do now?"

She did not look at me when she said, "The first thing we need to do is find the cheapest inn and get a room."

We walked through the village searching for an inn. Nessa stopped and spoke to an old woman, then Nessa led the way for a few blocks until we reached the inn. It was an old rundown building constructed of brown brick. The white paint on the window frames and doors was faded and peeling. We managed to get the last room available. The room had a small window and very little natural light. It was so small that it could barely hold two cots, but it would have to do. The floor creaked with every step; we would need to be careful walking around when Kat was asleep. After all that she had been through, she was becoming more sensitive to noise and sometimes jumped at the slightest sound.

The next day, I got a job at the docks helping to unload goods from ships. My hours were from dawn until dusk. By the end of the day, my back turned into knots, but I didn't care. I was happy to be working and making money to help support us. Nessa found a meadow nearby where she could pick plants and started making her healing medicines. On my days off, I helped Nessa sell her goods. A vendor who sold heating oil and candles had let Nessa use some space in his booth to sell her medicines.

One day, when I was helping Nessa sell her medicine, I was holding a fussy babbling Kat. The air was hotter and more humid, and people seemed to be moving at a snail's pace. The smell of the sea hung in the air and clung to everything and everyone. I looked up to see an old man who looked like he could barely stand getting pushed to the ground by a girl wearing a green sash. I handed over Kat to Nessa and ran to help the old man.

Once the old man was up on his feet, I yelled at the girl, "Hey, didn't anyone ever teach you to respect the elderly?"

Then the girl stopped in her tracks. She laughed and said, "I am exceedingly older than him, girly. Do you know who I am? "

I stepped in front of the old man just in case she wasn't done with him. She took her cloak off, throwing it to the side. She had olive skin, flaming red hair that reached a little below her shoulders, and red eyes with fire in them. She wore long pants the color of dark ash with a brown leather sleeveless top that had a high collar with gold buckles and black heeled boots. She had dark gray scales on her arms and some on the side of her face that trailed down her neck. She looked no older than her late twenties perhaps. Her arms were muscular and covered in scars that she wore with pride. She took a few steps closer to me, and she smelled of smoke and ash.

She then hissed and said, "What are you going to do about it, little girl, against me, the Great Fire Dragoness Kyra?" She pushed me to the ground with a smug grin, flashing a spiteful smile at me while walking away.

I could almost smell her smugness. I stood up and ran, pushing her with all my strength. When I did that, she went flying into the building in front of her, hitting it with a thud and leaving a slight indent where she'd hit it. I looked at my arms in shock not knowing my own strength.

She started to laugh and then said, "Little girl wants to fight?"

She pulled out a golden sword as Nessa threw my staff to me. By now, a crowd was forming. She struck first, trying to slash me, but missed. Then she kicked me in the gut and tripped me, causing me to fall to the ground on my back. She slashed at my throat, but I blocked it with my staff and knocked her off her feet. I stood up as she jumped to her feet. We charged at each other. My staff had changed into a scythe. I swung at her, and she attempted to block it with her sword. Her sword shattered like a rock thrown through a window. The crowd stood there in astonishment. Gasps could be heard in the crowd.

She stood there, wide-eyed, for a moment, then snarled, "You'll pay for that, you wench."

A giant wall of water formed from a nearby fountain and hit her hard, throwing her backward on the ground. A handsome tall man appeared, who was extremely pale with pearly white hair and glowing bright blue eyes. He wore a navy-blue shirt with a light blue vest over it, with black pants and boots. He looked to be about the same age as the red-headed girl. He carried himself with elegance and pride, as if his self-confidence had no limit. He looked strong and muscular. His skin was flawless, with fewer scales than the girl.

Enraged, he yelled, "Really? Kyra, for being over one hundred years old, you still act like a foolish child."

"What I do is none of your business, Liam," the red-haired girl Kyra said.

Liam's voice dropped, but it still seemed loud because all the noise around us ceased. Every word that came from his mouth was cold, with venom and anger seeping in from every letter. "So you barge into my territory unannounced, get into a fight, attack my people, and you dare tell me that this is none of my damn business?" Liam said.

Kyra stood there silently, trying to think of the right words, because she did not want to make him angrier than he already was. "Just because you are my fiancee, doesn't mean you are in charge here."

Then Liam hit Kyra with another wall of water, a little softer than the last time, before turning to me. Liam sighed and said in his normal voice, "I personally apologize for my associate, Ms. . .?"

"I am Bora, from Arm," I said with pride, as I noticed him studying me while the crowd whispered among themselves.

"Come along, Kyra. We're leaving,"

And they went on their way. Kyra turned back and glared at me before returning her attention back to Liam. I walked back to Nessa, and we returned to our room.

In a harsh voice, Nessa asked, "Why did you tell people that you are from Arm?"

I turned to her and said, "People will eventually find out. I prefer to be judged now rather than them finding out later and losing their trust. "What did he mean by territory?"

Nessa was changing Kat's diaper and said, "King Maverick came up with the idea to make it easier for him to rule. So he separated the land into territories and gave the territories to his board of governors to manage and then to report back to him.

"Now it is late. It is time for bed."

It took me a while before I was able to close my eyes and finally drift off to sleep.

CHAPTER 3

Task at Hand

NOT MORE THAN TWO DAYS had passed when a letter arrived at the inn. The letter was from Liam, asking if I would be interested in a job he had for me. Since I had proved myself capable of being a worthy opponent, Liam thought I would be able to complete the task at hand. The letter said that he needed me to go retrieve a book from the abandoned library in Vor Langer, which had long ago suffered from a large earthquake, making the town unlivable. He would pay me handsomely along with providing a small team to help make sure that I would return unharmed. I told Nessa I was working overtime and would be staying on the boat for a few days. I felt horrible lying to her, but I did not want Nessa to worry about me. The next day at work, I told her boss I needed to take a week off because I had a personal issue that needed to be taken care of. I got the feeling he didn't want to know why because he did not question it.

That morning, I left with my staff, wearing an old black cloak. Before I left, I kissed Kat on the head and gave Nessa a hug.

Nessa asked, "Why are you taking your staff?"

I replied, "After the incident with the redhead, you can prepare for the worst but can always hope for the best," before leaving.

I was on my way. I walked to a bar called Ses Larmes with a teardrop sign above the door. It didn't look like anything special from the outside other than being an old brick building that was on the bad side of town. However, my mind quickly changed as a man came flying through the window shattering it into pieces. I ducked, barely missing getting hit by the man. He landed unconscious on the ground behind me. He looked strong, and his forearms were the size of a grown man's thighs. I took a deep breath and put on a serious face to hide my fear. I pushed open the door and walked in, but I couldn't stop my knees from buckling with every step I took. It reeked of nasty tobacco smoke that was so strong it made my eyes water. I struggled to hold back tears. My throat and lungs burned as I scanned the room looking for an available seat. One thing was obvious: the place was packed. Most of the customers were men, but there were a few women who were covered in henna and tattoos. Some of the tattoos actually moved. There was a man sitting at the bar who had a snake slithering up one arm and then moving to the other. Along the walls hung a number of signs with rules written on them. Some signs said to leave your weapons at the door, but since this place was full of thieves, no one followed the rules. One said that anyone who disrespects a woman will be chucked out of a window, and many others said similar things. At least, I now knew why that guy was chucked out of the window. All eyes fell on me as I walked by, but as soon as I walked past them, they continued doing what they had been doing, be it arm wrestling, gambling, or pounding drinks.

I sat at the bar next to a man with an unusually long neck who looked like he was in despair. He was the only one there other than me who didn't have a drink.

I said, "Hello. How are you?" to the man with the very long neck, and the bartender looked at me as if I were a mad woman.

The bartender then said, "Now, are you going to buy something to drink, or are you going to waste my time?"

"I am sorry. I'll have water."

The bartender looked at me and shook his head. "Are you sure?"

"Yes, just water will be great. Thanks."

The bartender shrugged and said, "Fine. Your funeral," before walking away.

I waited a couple of minutes before he returned. When he came back, he placed a cup of disgusting dark brown muddy water in front of me. I thanked him again but did not touch the water. I waited all day, and when evening came and went, I was still waiting but no one from my team arrived. Soon it was only me and the bartender. Sometime during the night, the man with the long neck who was next to me had disappeared.

I was thinking of leaving when the door slammed open, and two people wearing brown cloaks walked in. They took off their cloak hoods: one was a young woman, and the other was a young man. They were almost identical to each other. The young woman was very beautiful, and the young man was handsome. They both had long dark brownish red hair, and both had light brown eyes. The woman wore a long-sleeved white shirt with brown shorts and high brown boots. The young man wore a short-sleeved light blue shirt with long brown pants and short brown boots. They both sat next to me, not saying a word. The three of us sat there in silence.

Then the door slammed open, almost breaking it off its hinges. All three of us jumped, and the young man fell off his stool and onto the floor. The older man who had just walked in walked up to us and showed us a map that said "Vor Langer."

None of us said anything as we grabbed our things and followed the man out of the bar.

Outside I said, "If we are going to work together, we should at least know each other's names."

The girl said, "Like I care enough to even remember your name."

"Now that is rude, sis. Sorry about her. I'm Amos, and this is Avery."

Avery hissed out at Amos in an irritated voice, "I am not rude. I just don't care." She then turned her attention to the man with the cloak and said, "Let's get on with this, and you know our names; now tell us yours."

"I am Bora. Nice to meet you all.

The man in the cloak did not turn around or stop his brisk pace; he only responded, "You can call me Cozbie."

We walked out of the town being guided by the moon. I looked back one more time, then thought this was for Nessa and Kat and continued to walk. We headed south for two days. I watched Amos trip, stumble, and get hurt more than it was humanly possible. We stopped and rested when we reached a forest called Mammoth. The forest was beautiful, and everything was giant in size. In comparison, we were the size of ants.

As we walked on the mossy ground, Cozbie stopped and said, "Be careful where you step. Some of this land is sacred, so keep to the trail."

Up in a tree was a creature that looked like the strangest bird I had ever seen. It was about two feet long with a round head and two large black eyes that made it horrifyingly cute. Its feathers had varied colors of brown and gray. It had several long tail feathers and stared at us as it sat up in its nest. Then out of nowhere, another one appeared swooping down, opening its mouth very wide before catching a giant moth. It returned to the nest to share with its mate.

Amos stopped and said, "That is a Great Potoo. Legends say that, if you hear its cry, your soul will be sucked out of your body."

"No, Amos. That's preposterous. The Great Potoo legends say that they were once babies that were abandoned in the forest and transformed into what you see in front of you. Or another legend is about a girl who was cursed because she stole a witch's lover. All these legends had started from their haunting cries." As Avery walked on, she said, "Keep up, you two," as she continued ahead of us.

We continued to walk a few miles more into the forest. Avery abruptly stopped and looked around worriedly.

"What's wrong?" I asked, concerned.

"Where is Amos?" She then yelled for Amos, "If this is a joke, come out right now, because this isn't funny," but there was no response.

Then, there were footsteps behind us followed by the sound of branches breaking. I turned around and had my staff ready, not knowing what was coming. Amos fell from behind the bushes behind us. He scrambled to his feet while Avery let out a sigh of relief and ran over to help him up.

"Where did you run off to, Amos?" I asked.

Amos finished brushing himself off before replying, "I stayed back to use the bathroom."

"Please don't tell me you went to the bathroom on sacred land," Avery said.

Amos looked confused and said, "What about sacred land?"

Avery replied, "You know the sacred land Cozbie told us to avoid."

Amos still had a blank expression on his face and said, "You know I don't pay attention, and that is just an old wives' tale. So no need to worry."

Avery opened her mouth and was about to reply when a putrid smell filled the air. The only thing that I could think of comparing it to was rotten vegetables and sewage that had long gone bad; this smell would be it. Every time we opened our mouths we gagged because we could taste it. Then a gray creature jumped down from a tree where we were standing. The creature was tall. It had talon-like claws, a mouth with teeth as sharp as knives, an extremely long tongue on its abdomen, a single eye where its head should have been, and gray rough skin. Its shape was in human form, but it looked nothing like a human.

"What is that thing?" Avery yelled while covering her nose and mouth.

Cozbie put one of his oversized hands over his mouth and said something no one could make out other than the beginning of the word "Jum."

"What about the Jum?" I asked, overwhelmed by the foul smell.

"No! It's a Juma. Oh no! I can taste it," Cozbie said, taking his hand off his mouth so they could hear him better, but he was now gagging and trying not to vomit.

While this was going on, the Juma was now circling us like a predator surrounding his prey. The Juma jumped on Amos, pinning him to the ground. Amos struggled under its weight, and they continued to wrestle on the ground. I turned to Avery and Cozbie who were watching this go down.

"Shouldn't we do something to help him?" I asked.

"What is the likelihood the Juma will attack us after it finishes off my idiot brother?"

"There is a very big chance," Cozbie said.

"What do you think will happen if we run away while it's distracted with Amos?" Avery said.

"Are you really alright with leaving your own brother for dead?" Cozbie asked.

Avery turned around and said, "He will be missed."

Amos and I looked at Avery, our eyes widening in utter shock.

"It's a joke, Amos," she said.

Amos yelled back, "It better be a joke, you jerk. I am not only your brother but your twin. Do you know how much trouble you and your trainwreck of a love life had put me through?"

"Hey, don't bring my love life into this," Avery yelled back.

"Why not when you drag me into it all the time?" he said.

By this time, Amos and the Juma were no longer on the ground but still engaged in hand-to-hand combat.

"Enough. Now, Bora, do you see where its belly button is?" Cozbie said.

I nodded and gave him a confused look. Avery took out a dark wood bow and started firing arrows at the Juma. The first three hit it in his side causing it to turn its attention to her. The arrows had bounced off its hard, thick skin. When she picked up a fairly big rock the size of her hand and threw it at the Juma, the rock hit it in the eye, and in its irritation, it threw Amos off to the side. It got up and came running toward Avery and tried to swipe her with its claws, which she dodged. It took me a second to find its belly button. It was right above its mouth in the middle of its belly. From far away, it looked somewhat like a nose. I held my staff and ran toward the Juma while it was distracted by Avery. I made sure to hit it exactly where its belly button was. Suddenly, everything stopped and there was only silence. Then came screaming, loud blood-curdling screaming. I had struck the Juma right in its belly button, which resulted in my staff poking out the other side. When I pulled it out, a river of dark green thick blood came rushing out. The Juma screamed and tried to close the gaping hole where its belly button used to be. After a couple of minutes, the Juma struggled to stop the blood from coming out and collapsed on the ground good and dead.

Avery ran over to her brother to make sure he was ok. "Ugh, it got blood all over my boots," Avery said.

"Aren't Juma supposed to be covered with red hair?" Amos asked.

Cozbie said, "It was an adolescent. Its mother was probably killed given that it couldn't hunt properly."

"What do you mean by 'couldn't hunt properly'?" I asked.

Cozbie said with a cracking voice, "Juma hunt by sneaking up and cutting off their prey's legs so they can't run away. Then they cut off their arms so they can't fight back, and then they eat them."

"How do you know about this?" I asked.

Cozbie said, "I read about them in a book."

I was about to ask him more questions, but he started to walk away with the twins following behind him.

"Shouldn't we at least bury the body?" I asked.

Avery turned on her heels and walked toward me and said, "Let's get something straight. You have remorse, you die; you go out of your way for someone, you die. Do I make myself clear?,"

Her face was close to mine when I said, "Yes it's clear you care for no one but yourself."

She slapped me right across the face and walked away.

We continued to walk through the giant forest. Amos now moved more carefully and stuck to the middle of the path. He did not want to repeat what had just happened.

Avery said to Amos, "No more bathroom breaks."

"Don't be so tense, sis. This is how these things go. We take a job in a new place; almost die by a monster. Then we leave and face another fight another day in a new place."

"This isn't like your stupid adventure books, Amos. This is real life."

Before he could reply, the ground under us started to shake, and a hole formed in the path. We all ran to hold on to something. Amos grabbed on to a vine, trying to reach Avery's hand, when something that resembled a scorpion's tail wrapped around her leg and dragged her into the hole.

"Avery," Amos yelled, running after her, but was stopped by Cozbie.

Cozbie said, "She is probably already dead. You're just wasting your time, boy."

Amos turned to me, "I am going after her. Will you help save her? Please help!"

When Amos said that, memories flashed of my encounter with the thieves: the pleading boy on his knees, the two men and I in that dark stone house with small windows and the blocked door, the night of the Minotaur raid and people screaming and pleading for help, all the bloodshed, all the lives that were lost, how I had failed all of them. What snapped me out of my thoughts was Amos's shaking voice.

"Please. This is my sister. I am going after her whether you help me or not."

I said nothing but nodded. He jumped down the hole, and I followed. We landed on hard but loose dirt. I landed on my feet, and Amos landed on his bottom. Amos pulled out a small torch from his cloak pocket and lit it. The light from the torch glowed brightly as we made our way through the dark cave. I walked on my tiptoes so I could be as quiet as possible. We walked for about half a mile when we heard a roar.

I turned to Amos. "You go find Avery, and I'll hold off the creature."

We split up. The beast pounced on top of me and tried to bite my face, but I stopped it with the staff. I heard a baby roar and turned my head and saw a baby manticore. Its fur looked fluffy and soft. It had a stubby, small scorpion tail and teeny tiny wings. I was eye to eye with the mom. I used my strength to push her off me, and the mom roared again. She had the body and head of a medium-sized lion, large side wings, and a scorpion tail. Then a stalactite fell from the roof of the cave. I ran and pushed the mom out of the way. The stalactite fell to where the mom had been and crashed into pieces. She stopped and looked at me. I felt something climbing up my leg. I looked down and saw the baby manticore holding on tight. I walked over to the mom and handed her cub to her. I picked up my staff and walked away. I immediately heard yelling, and before I could blink, the mom stung something, and it fell to the ground. I saw that the mom had stung Amos with her tail, and now his body was on the floor and he was unconscious. Avery showed up unharmed shortly afterward, which was good. We followed the mama to the center of the cave, while Avery and I dragged her brother by his arms. When we reached the center, we saw two more cubs. Avery picked up one, and the other sat on Amos's limp body. After Amos had awakened, the mama showed us a trail we could follow and make our way out of the cave.

Avery said, "The manticore pulled me down the hole but took one look at me and walked away. The hole was too high for me to reach so I went looking for another way out. I think she thought I was a goat, and she did not want a fight with cubs nearby."

We made our way back to the trail. We found Cozbie and continued on our way.

Over the next day, Cozbie refused to talk to any of us, started to smell like something rotting, and was attracting a lot of flies. He hadn't eaten or drunk at all since we had started on our journey. Amos and I became close friends. Avery, on the other hand, I like to think our friendship snuck up on her. After another day and a half of walking and seeing Amos get hurt more than I thought was humanly possible, we arrived at Vor Langer.

Vor Langer was an old large library that was abandoned after the town was destroyed sixty-three years ago by an enormous earthquake. The north and south wings of the library had collapsed, but the main library was fully intact and had two giant wooden doors with elaborate carvings. It was here we were advised that the book in question would be located. We shoved the two massive doors open and walked in. The inside of what would have been the main building was cluttered and dusty with the largest spider webs I had ever seen. It looked so much bigger from the inside than it did on the outside. There were books and scrolls scattered everywhere, including all over the floor. Amos screamed at the top of his lungs, and we all turned to him. I lifted my staff, ready to fight, not sure what Amos had seen.

We all stood still afraid to move, and I asked Amos, "What is going on?"

He stood there with a blank expression on his face and said, "What"?

"Why did you scream?" Avery asked, with concern in her voice.

"I wanted to see if my voice would echo," he said, while rubbing the back of his neck in embarrassment.

Avery slapped herself on the forehead in irritation and said, "Sometimes I wonder if you have a working brain cell in that head of yours."

Cozbie shook his head disapprovingly, and I patted his back trying to make him feel better.

Before we split up to start looking for the book, I said, "It is an old brown leather book with a sword and a dragon embossed in gold leaf on the front and back cover. In the middle of the cover is a box that holds the name 'R. Becket.'"

We made a plan to spread out; each of us took a diffcrent sec-tion. I advised everyone to look through the bookshelves in each of our sections first and then go through the books on the tables and the books on the floor. With any luck, we would be able to find the book and be on our way. I started in the farthest part of the library and suddenly realized that brown leather books were the most pop-ular. After hours of looking, I finished my section. Amos had also just finished, and we both helped Avery finish looking through her section. We found Cozbie sitting on the floor, sleeping with his back against the bookshelves. I walked over to the next bookshelf. This one was different, much smaller, and was made of marble, and after only a few minutes, I pulled a faded brown leather book from the shelf. Its front and back cover had a sword and dragon and in faded gold leaf was "R. Becket." The book was old and ripped with crisp yellow pages.

I yelled, "I found it!"

Avery and Amos both cheered.

"Let's get out of here and let's go deliver it to Liam," I said, smiling.

Amos and Avery looked at each other, then at me confused.

Avery said, "What are you talking about? We were hired by a tradesman we know to retrieve the book."

Amos chimed in, "He sent us a letter."

He showed me the letter that he'd had in his pocket. I examined it, and it was exactly the same letter that I had received. The only difference was the signature at the bottom.

We then heard a loud slam. We all turned our heads and saw that the large library doors were now shut. Cozbie gave us a wide evil smile. His eyes rolled to the back of his head before they fell out of their sockets and onto the floor. He dropped his cloak, and all his clothes were stained with dried blood. His body went limp as he fell backward and hit the floor with a loud thud. His large stomach started to move as if it were being pushed on from the inside. A large cut appeared, and it seemed to be getting bigger by the minute. Then two bony hands reached out through the large cut from inside of what was Cozbie's body, and slowly it started to pull itself out. First, the head appeared, then the shoulders and torso, soon its legs, and before we knew it, it was standing in front of us.

Once the creature was out, we were able to see who he was or should I say who she was. She had white hair, but the dried blood had turned it to a garnet color. She was small and boney. Her face had a hollow and sunken appearance. She wore a torn black shirt and pants that looked to be two sizes too big. Obviously, she had taken them from her last victim. Her body looked twisted; her legs were turned to the side as she walked forward. Her face was covered with dried blood, her grin was wider than it had been minutes before, and her teeth were pointed and yellow. Her eyes were small and black. The bottom of her clothes appeared to be a greenish- black pigment that looked familiar. At that moment, everything about the Juma incident made sense.

I spoke as calmly as I could and said, "The bottom of your pants has dried Juma blood on them. It was the same kind that was on Avery's boots. The Juma must have attacked us because you had killed its mother and it picked up your scent, and Amos was in front of you when the Juma attacked. It wasn't aiming for him—it was you."

The hag cackled. "Yes. I killed its mother. I didn't want it getting in our way. I did not realize it had a baby. Too bad Amos just happened to be collateral. I really was hoping for his demise."

Amos grabbed his spear while his sister pulled out her bow and arrow. The hag said, "teine," a fireball suddenly appeared and she threw it hitting a bookshelf, which fell on Avery. When it did, Avery shot her arrow up and the arrow ended up hitting a chandelier, which then fell on Amos. I tried to hit the hag with my staff, but she used her magic and sent me flying backward, knocking over two more bookshelves. I looked up, and the hag had another fireball ready to throw at Amos who was knocked out from the chandelier falling on him. Avery was trying to get the bookshelf off herself. I struggled to my feet, scythe now in hand. I knew I had to protect them no matter what. I picked up a book off the floor and threw it at her. She turned her head 360° and just stared at me. I walked to the center of the room. The hag turned her head back around and walked toward me. Somehow her smile was getting wider than it already was. Suddenly the wind began blowing, and it started to get windier with every step she took.

"Why?" I asked.

"Why what?" the hag replied.

"Why did you put in all this effort just to lure us here?" I said.

When she stood right in front of me, a tornado formed around us, but it was not moving. It was a barrier to keep Amos and Avery away from us. My arm felt strange. I looked down and saw that my right arm from the tip of my fingers to my elbow was covered in light gray scales.

"What's wrong? Cat got your tongue?" the hag said mockingly. "Why don't I tell you a little story? Once upon a time, there was a very beautiful girl who got everything she wanted in life. Then a horrible oversized lizard showed up and took it all away from the girl. The lizard had cursed the poor girl. For many years, the girl suffered with her curse, til one day she saw you, Bora. You are my revenge on him. You and all your disgusting half breeds are on the brink of extinction, and I would be more than happy to help with that." She pointed at my lower arm covered in scales.

"Try me, you hag," I said, raising my scythe ready to strike.

"Why, you little—" the hag said, and threw a fireball at me, but it missed and ended up spinning around us in the tornado.

It went flying and shot up to the ceiling and broke through the roof of the building, leaving a hole in it. I ran as fast as I could, swung my scythe, and the witch's arm was cut clean off. In a matter of seconds, the fight was over. Her body lay there not moving. A lot of blood was coming out from where the missing appendage had been. She was dead, or so I thought. The wind around us stopped blowing. My lower right arm was still covered in light gray scales. I looked over and saw Avery was out from under the bookshelf and was struggling to get the chandelier off her brother before it crushed him.

I told her, "Move out of the way," and I picked it up with one hand.

My arm with the scales lifted it up as if it were a feather. As I threw it off to the side, Avery helped Amos up, and we heard slow clapping. We looked up to where the fireball had left a hole in the roof, and I saw a familiar face.

CHAPTER 4

Returning Home

KYRA WAS STANDING ON TOP of the roof peering down at us from the hole in the ceiling, with an amused look on her face. She jumped down from the roof landing on her feet. Her scratched-up boots clicked on the floor with every step she took toward us.

Amos's jaw dropped, and he said, "Great Dragoness, what are you doing here?"

Kyra just ignored him and walked toward me and said, "That was quite a show you put on, humans and half breed." She studied my arm. "What actually are you?"

I put on my best mocking smile, curtsied teasingly, and said, "Like I told you before, I'm Bora, a simple girl from Arm."

She walked over, picked up the book that we were sent to retrieve that was lying on the floor, and put it in a shoulder bag. "I saw you in the forest and decided to follow you, considering you have a reputation for finding trouble." At that, she paused, glared at me, and said, "Why don't I believe you're a simple girl from Arm? For right now, this is what we are going to do. I am going to bring you all to Liam, and he can decide what to do with you, Dora from Arm."

I snapped at her, "I am not going anywhere with you. Also my name is Bora, not Dora."

She sighed and said, "Fine. You want to do this the hard way," before walking over to me and throwing me over her shoulder with little to no effort.

As we exited the library, I looked back one more time and the hag's body was gone. Kyra walked down the steps of the library entrance.

"How do you know Kyra?" Avery asked.

"Well, you see, I kicked the Great Dragoness Kyra's butt in a fight," I said.

Kyra stopped dead in her tracks, dropping me, but I caught myself with my arms and rolled and landed on my feet.

Kyra said, "I did not lose a fight with you. I lost a fight with Liam."

"Is that what you tell people so you don't ruin your reputation with your boyfriend?" Kyra snapped back, "He is my fiance, so watch your mouth, Dora."

If looks could kill, I should have died a slow and painful death by the way Kyra was looking at me. Once we walked away from the library, Kyra shifted into her dragon form. She was enormous; she was bigger than a two-story house. She had dark ash scales with two horns on her head and two enormous, long thin wings with red scales at the tips of her wings. We all climbed on her back. Avery handed me my staff, and Kyra instructed us to sit in the dip between her shoulder blades. We flew for a few hours and only stopped at night to sleep. That night, before we went to bed, Amos whipped up a pot of stew for supper. Kyra had started the fire with ease as she used her hand to mold a fireball and put it under the firewood. Within seconds, a fire blazed.

"Can all dragons do that?" I asked.

"Do what?" she asked, confused.

"Create fire."

"No. I'm a fire dragon; I can do fire manipulation. My breed lived in some of the hottest climates of this world. Liam, on the other hand, is a water dragon; he does water manipulation. Liam is quite comfortable spending time under water. Theron is a time dragon; he can move time forward, and he sees glimpses of the future. King Maverick is a thunder dragon; he can summon storms and harness lighting. His original breed live in the mountainous areas. Witches, on the other hand, can do other types of magic, except transformation."

"Is that why the hag used the corpses of her last victims to disguise herself?" I asked.

"Yes, that is correct. Do you know what therianthropy is?" she asked.

"Yes. Therianthropy is when humans can transform into an animal and back into human form at will."

Krya added, "They always transform into the same animal. There are very few people in history who have this gift, or some may say curse."

"Supper is ready," Amos called out.

We all looked at each other reluctantly. The stew had a disgusting brown color and smelled worse than the dead guy the hag had emerged from. We all were quite surprised because the stew actually tasted much better than it looked and smelled. Kyra and Amos fell asleep right after eating, and I lay there trying to figure out which one of them was snoring louder. Avery went out to get more firewood. I sat up looking at the stars. It was cold, yet I seemed to have a high tolerance for the cold and the stew helped to keep Avery and Amos warm. I wondered how Nessa and Kat were doing in my absence. After a while, I heard footsteps. I turned my head and saw Avery walking my way after she had put more firewood in the fire. She sat down next to me. There was a long moment of silence before she spoke.

"You barely ate. It is actually one of Amos's better meals."

I stared at her wide-eyed and asked, "Why do you let him cook?"

"Amos is good at some things, but cooking is not one of them. I really hate cooking and he seems to enjoy it, so sometimes I have to hold my nose when I eat. I don't mind.

"I want him to know, no matter what, I have faith in him. I mean, you met the clumsy guy. What do you think would happen if he was in charge of the fire?"

We looked at each other and said in unison, "He would probably set himself on fire."

We laughed, and Avery said, "In all seriousness, he has saved my life multiple times. How long are you planning on staying in Bateau?" she asked.

"I'm staying for a while," I said. "How about you and Amos?"

"I think Amos and I are going to stick around for a while, too."

The next thing I knew,, I was fast asleep.

At dawn, we packed up camp and Kyra transformed back into her dragon form. We all climbed up on her back, and in a few hours, we were back in Bateau where Kyra led us toward the water. We stopped in front of a large Mediterranean white marble home. It had two faded wooden doors with a mermaid carved on each side, and both of them were holding a conch shell that was cut in half when the door was opened. We left Avery and Amos on the beach as we headed in. Kyra wasted no time shoving both doors open with a bang, not knowing her own strength. We walked right into a big room with a swimming pool-sized hole in the middle of the room and a light blue couch. There was a wooden table with a clear glass vase full of seashells instead of flowers.

Kyra jumped on the couch and said, "We need to wait for Liam to get back."

I was about to ask her where he was when a hand grabbed the edge of the pool. Within a flash, Liam was out of the pool as he grabbed a towel and turned to Kyra. That was when I noticed that he had a fishing net tattoo on his left side that had a glass bottle with a note in it over his heart that said "Kyra."

He sighed in irritation, putting his hand on the bridge of his nose, and said, "You know it's rude to come into someone's house unannounced."

Kyra put on a cocky grin. "I live here too sometimes, so this house is as much mine as it is yours."

Liam was about to say something but paused and said, "Fair enough."

It was obvious he was still a little frustrated. Kyra put her hand up to his face cupping his cheek and kissed him.

As she pulled away from him, Kyra said, "Don't be mad. I love you, and I have something interesting to show you."

Liam still looked irritated, blushing from Kyra's kiss. Kyra grabbed my arm and pointed to the scales that were still there.

Liam's eyes widened in shock as he took my arm and started to inspect it. "What are you? Where are you from? Who was your mother?" he said.

I told him about waking up under the tree and about following the cat, finding Nessa, and my time in the village of Arm; how we left the village of Arm after it was attacked and burnt down to the ground; and how we had taken a boat and our mishap with the sea monster; how we arrived at Bateau; how I received a letter of employment for the collection of an old book; then how Kyra had found us at Vor Langer and brought me back to see him.

Liam and Kyra both looked bewildered. There were several times when both of them opened their mouths to say something but couldn't find the words.

After a long silence, Kyra finally spoke and said to Liam, "We have to take her to see King Maverick."

"Are you crazy? Do you know what Maverick would do to us if we bring an outsider to the meeting?" Liam said.

"Do you know what he'd do if he found out we were keeping this secret from him?" Kyra replied.

Liam remained silent for a moment, then sighed before nodding. He looked at me and said, "Don't make me regret this decision."

I smiled and went over to thank him, but he immediately pushed me away and said, "Go put bandages on your arm to hide those scales for now. We'll bring you to the next dragon meeting, but know that if it all goes to hell, it is your fault, Kyra."

I looked at them and asked, "What can you tell me about King Maverick?"

Liam shook his head and stared at Kyra. "Maverick is the king and is also dragon-like us," he said.

Kyra cut in and said, "In other words, no one would go against him."

Liam cleared his throat and said, "You don't know the history of this world?"

I shook my head no.

"I will explain it to you," Liam said.

Kyra let out a huff. "Great. Be prepared to be bored."

Liam gave Kyra a glance that made her shut up and said, "Like it or not Kyra, our history is important. It helps us learn from our mistakes in the past so we can learn to improve in the present and the future."

Kyra rolled her eyes. "Yea. I'm going to prepare some food and drinks," she said and left the room.

"Can you explain how half breeds come to be, Liam?" I asked.

"I have heard many different stories. There is a story that has been passed down for hundreds of years of a young woman who was to be married to a very desirable wealthy baron. This wealthy baron had many women suitors, but he chose a young sweet girl. This angered one of the women who then hired a power witch to turn the young sweet girl into a dragon. Only this young girl was already pregnant with her soon-to-be husband's child. Her soon-to-be husband was told that she had run away with a different man to be married. The young girl, now turned dragon, gave birth to a human baby girl. As the girl grew, she later found that she could transform to a dragon and back to her human form."

Liam paused and continued. "Thousands of years ago, true dragons lived peaceful solitary lives in every corner of this world. Since they spent much of their life alone, their numbers were few. Humans and Minotaurs were always fighting over land. The human population grew at great numbers, putting more stress on their already strained relationship. One day, the Minotaurs attacked a small village before dawn and killed every single person in the village. That had happened over five hundred years ago and was the beginning of the 1st War.

"The first woman soldier gathered all the nations under her. She is known as Queen Phoenix, the first ruler and queen of the Inue, who rose from the ashes of war. Halfway through the war, Queen Phoenix, shortly after her coronation, wrote a peace treaty. To make it official, she agreed to a marriage arrangement between Minotaur General Pantoran and herself. Unfortunately, a lot of people on both sides were against this union. The day of the wedding was a public event, and just when they were exchanging vows, a poisonous arrow came out of nowhere and hit her."

Kyra yelled, "How about the part that Phoenix was constantly looked down on by her fellow soldiers when she first joined the army? The fact that their side was only winning because of her gifted abilities to lead and how she was unmatched by anyone with a sword and bow? And how about when Phoenix and Minotaur General Pantoran, before he became General Pantoran, got separated from their squadrons by a band of thieves? They were handcuffed to each other and had to travel together until they were able to steal the keys and escape. How about, when Phoenix realized that Minotaurs and humans wanted the same thing, she lost her fighting spirit to continue the war? Or the fact that the poisoned arrow did not kill her immediately, and she fought for her life in the medical wing for over seventeen hours before she finally passed away from the poison?"

"Wow, Kyra, you sure are passionate when it comes to Queen Phoenix," I said.

Kyra smiled, "How could I not be? She was awesome. Queen Phoenix didn't take crap from anyone; her death is still one of the biggest mysteries to this day because no one knows who fired the poisonous arrow."

Liam continued, "Sadly she died and her twin sister Zena became queen, and the peace treaty was invalidated. The marriage never happened, and a few days later, Minotaur General Pantoran was killed. Queen Zena became queen, but she blamed the dragons for not fighting with the humans against the Minotaurs. Unknown to the dragons, she secretly ordered them all to be hunted down and killed. As the war progressed, Queen Zena, who had been outraged by her sister's death, did whatever she could to prolong the war. Queen Zena married General Minos after becoming queen, and he continually encouraged her to continue the war. The war continued for sixty-three years before King Theodore, Queen Zena's grandson, became king and he signed a peace treaty ending the 1st War.

"At that time, the true dragons had all been killed off. King Theodore, having a soft spot for the half breeds, gave us high ranking positions in the government. King Theodore was murdered by Arnold the Conqueror, and due to him having no living relatives, Arnold the Conqueror became king. After Arnold became king, he declared that the half breeds were now not considered to be human and would now only be considered dragons. So he put a price on our heads and made us fight for our lives in the colosseum. Many of us went into hiding, and almost all were found to have lost their lives. There are only a handful left alive today, but we believe that there may be some dragons still hiding in their human form."

Suddenly the smell of something burning filled the air, causing Kyra to stop listening for a few seconds before running back into the kitchen.

Liam continued. "King Arnold's the conqueror son and heir King Fredick then took over the throne. Then King Fredick's son King Lowel became king. King Lowel never wanted to be king. He was shy, weak, and sickly. Sada had befriended him, and he gladly abdicated the throne to her making her Queen Sada. Queen Sada ruled for over forty years before she passed away. King Maverick then claimed the throne at that time, and he has ruled for almost twenty years."

We continued talking for a while, and then Liam told me they would come and get me when it was time for the meeting. Kyra returned and helped me wrap my arm in bandages so no one could see my scales, and I left.

After my meeting with Liam, I went on my way and met back up with Amos and Avery who were on the beach waiting for me. When we arrived at the inn, we saw Nessa washing bedsheets and Kat lying on a blanket on her back. Once Kat spotted me, she started giggling, alerting Nessa to my presence. The moment our eyes met, I saw she was angry, and she stomped over to me. Avery and Amos saw this and took a few steps back, leaving me to fight this battle alone. In a moment she was in front of me. She stepped closer until she was only a few inches from my face.

Nessa snarled, "Where were you, young lady?"

I nervously said, "What do you mean? I was working at the dock—"

She quickly cut me off. Nessa said with gritted teeth, "Liar! I stopped by the docks to bring you some food, and your boss told me you took time off! I want to know where you were!"

Nessa listened as I spoke, "I got a letter that said it was from Liam, and it said he would pay me handsomely to go and retrieve a book for him, but actually the letter was sent by an old hag to lure me and try and kill me at the library of Vor Langer. I defeated her, and apparently after my fight with Kyra, she had followed us, and she gave us a ride home." I unwrapped a strip of the bandage to show her the scales on my lower arm. Nessa's eyes widened as she looked at my arm. I then continued, "During my fight with the hag this happened. So when we arrived back in Bateau, Kyra dragged me to see Liam and tell him what had happened. I have been invited to go to the castle to see if I can get some answers about who or what I am. That brings us to where we are now, so now you're all caught up."

Nessa pointed at Avery and Amos and asked, "Who are those two?"

"Oh, that's Avery and Amos. They were also lured away with me. They will be staying with us if you don't mind?"

Nessa piped up and said, "Not only did you not get any money, but now we have two more mouths to feed. Am I correct?"

"Yeah, that's pretty much it, " I said, smiling at her nervously.

Nessa then said, "Are you crazy? We can barely afford ourselves, let alone these two. Bora, we are not running a charity here!"

Avery chimed in, "We can help out. I could help you make and sell your medicine, and Amos can—"

She was cut off by Amos who said, "I can cut and sell firewood."

"Ok. If that's what you want, I'm ok with it, but know if you accidentally axe off a limb, I'm not helping you," Avery said.

"Yeah," then he paused as he processed his sister's words in his head and said, "Wait—what?"

Nessa chuckled and said, "I like you, girl. You remind me of a less pretty younger me."

"Thank you. Hey, what do you mean by less pretty?" she said.

"No complaining, and help me with these sheets."

With that, I'd say everyone was getting along fairly well.

CHAPTER 5

Meeting of the Dragons

NO MORE THAN A WEEK later, I received a letter and substantial payment for my time from Liam. The letter told me when we would be leaving and when and where I'd meet up with Kyra and Liam. Liam had talked to my boss, who excused me from work while I was gone for the meeting, which I was very grateful for. A few days later, I walked on the warm yellow sand as I made my way to Liam and Kyra's home. I wasn't too far from their house when I noticed Liam standing in the water, knee deep. I walked over to him when I noticed he was in the middle of something, which happened to be Kyra throwing a fireball at him. I don't think she was aiming at this point because they were going every which way. One came flying straight at me, so I quickly ducked.

"Bora, duck," Liam yelled, which caused Kyra to look in my direction with a panicked expression.

I ducked in time as it hit the side of the rocky cliff behind me, leaving scorch marks in its wake. Liam and Kyra let out deep breaths after I managed to survive the fireball.

"How about we agree, no more fireballs before this gets out of hand?" Liam said.

"Yeah, that sounds good," Kyra said, while still looking at me and turning her attention back to Liam.

Kyra took this to her advantage, leaping toward Liam. Liam easily dodged her, causing Kyra to land on her stomach in the water. Liam caused the water to wrap around one of her legs tightly. He then tossed her a couple of feet in the air causing her to land farther out in the water forcing her a much longer swim back. Liam was walking out of the water and heading straight toward me. I thought Liam beat Kyra with little to no difficulty.

As he got closer, I quickly pulled myself out of my thoughts and said, "Sorry. . . am I interrupting something?"

Liam replied, "Not at all. We were just training."

He turned his attention to Kyra who was swimming back to the shore. Most of her hair was covering her face, so she had a hard time finding her way. She walked with one hand out in front of her, and with the other hand, she was trying to remove the hair that was stuck to her face. Liam grabbed a white towel from nearby and handed it to her. She grabbed it and started to dry herself off and fix her hair.

Liam said, "Ok, let's get going."

"What about me?" Kyra said.

"What about you?" Liam said.

Kyra snapped back with, "I'm soaking wet!"

Liam rolled his eyes and told her she'd be fine, that her clothes will dry on their way there. Kyra's expression changed. Liam recognized her anger and said, "Kyra, please calm down and don't make a scene."

Kyra snapped back and said, "Why should I be calm, Liam ? I have a right to be upset because you don't care if I get sick."

"Kyra, you are angry about nothing. You're not even wet now."

Kyra froze for a moment. Her hair was no longer dripping wet; her clothes were almost completely dry. She crossed her arms and pouted like a child and said, "It doesn't matter. I'm still mad at you."

Liam's normally sharp, cold blue eyes softened for a moment. It was a very short moment, and he secretly hoped I hadn't noticed. Liam walked over to Kyra and said, "I know I am not the warmest person. I often say things without any care about how people react to it. And yes, I know I don't show it, but at this moment, you are one of the most important things in my life. I lo—" he paused before saying, "I care a great deal about you," followed by a kiss on the forehead.

Kyra looked like she was on the verge of tears. Even I was shocked by the way Liam was acting. Liam was a straight-faced man who rarely, if ever, showed any genuine emotions or cared for anyone other than himself. He gave off the impression that nothing could faze him and he had not a single weakness. Yet for the first time in probably Liam's whole life, this was the closest he had ever gotten to being vulnerable.

After a moment, Liam snapped back to his regular self, saying, "Come on; let's go. We don't have all day."

He shifted into his beautiful silver-gray dragon form. Around his neck he had gills. All water dragons had gills for breathing underwater. Kyra and I climbed onto his big back, and we were off. Once we were in the air, Kyra started complaining that he was going too slow. I asked her why she wasn't flying. Kyra explained that Liam wanted her to keep me company.

"Kyra, can I ask you something?"

"Yeah, sure. What is it?" she said.

"What is it like to transform into a dragon?"

Kyra smiled and said, "It's like anything else. It takes time to learn, but after years of transforming, it's really very easy now. When you transform, you feel immense power and pride, as if nothing in this world can stop you. But we are also a lot easier to anger in our dragon form. Well, more specifically, my species of dragons—we are known to be more hotheaded than the others, and we are all very territorial. However, staying in our dragon form is quite draining both mentally and physically. So, being in our dragon forms for too long or constantly shifting back and forth without rest does make us weak."

Liam said, "You are going to have to be extremely careful once we arrive. You can't leave Kyra's or my side."

"Why?" I asked bluntly, not hiding my disappointment.

"Despite how Kyra and I act, not all dragons are as welcoming as we are," he said.

Kyra noticed and said, "It's because some of them have a strong dislike for humans."

She continued. "Well, you see, after the arena and bringing us to the brink of extinction, most of us are still holding a grudge."

"Now, Kyra, cut it out. You'll scare her," Liam said, before continuing, "There are three dragons you need to look out for in particular. The first one is King Maverick's sister. Her name is Ann, and out of all the people you will meet there, she is not the most sane, and that's putting it lightly. She can and will attack you for no reason, so make sure to never be alone with her even if you earn favor with the others. Never let your guard down around her. The second one is His Majesty King Maverick, who is the most influential person there, which goes without saying. Don't do anything to upset him, or it could cost you your life. Last is Theron," he said with a disapproving growl.

Kyra still had her usual cocky smile that I had grown accustomed to. She said, "Don't mind him one bit. He is not the biggest fan of Theron. Theron is the oldest dragon there, although he may not look like it."

"He is also a useless lazy drunk," Liam mumbled under his breath.

"Yes, you are right, Liam," Kyra said. "But you're forgetting one important detail. Out of everyone there, Theron knows everything.

He knows your deepest secret, so tell him the truth and only necessary information."

As we flew, the castle and the surrounding lands came into view. I was amazed at what I saw. Up on a tall mountainside stood a humongous castle built around and inside of the mountain. It was constructed of black granite. The land around it reminded me of a checkered board pattern. Surrounding the castle were huge metal gates to prevent any intruders. Behind the gates on the castle grounds were rows upon rows of black and white roses. In the rose garden, it looked like there was construction going on. Under the mountain was a small town. It looked modern and well managed. Surrounding the castle were dozens of armed guards in their shiny silver armor.

Kyra saw me observing the town as we flew over it, and she said in a fake fancy accent, "Well, Bora from Arm, may I introduce you to Perth, the city of the wealth and prestige." We both laughed at this, but it was cut short by the roaring of thunder. "Uh oh," Kyra said, in an unsure voice.

"What is it? Is something wrong?" I asked, concerned.

Kyra said, "Right now, we can only hope that King Maverick's sisters are upset and not him, because King Maverick is the kind of person you never want to upset."

We landed inside the rose garden on the stone walkway. Kyra jumped off Liam's back, while I carefully slid off. Liam shifted back into his human form and straightened his clothes and fixed his hair. As we made our way to the front entrance, the doors were twelve feet tall and stained black. On the doors were two silver dragons with a silver ring in their mouths that were door handles. Kyra grabbed the silver rings in the dragons' mouths and pushed the doors open. Well, I should say it was more like throwing the doors open with a bang. Liam started to lecture her about manners when a woman walking down the stairs headed toward us. She looked paler than the white roses outside and was very thin. She wore an oversized black dress with long bell sleeves. She wasn't wearing shoes and walked on her tiptoes as if she was walking on glass and one wrong move would leave her feet a bloody mess. Her hair was long, dark, and untidy. She had large doll-like eyes with big bags under them. She looked like a walking corpse. When she finally spoke, it was in a quiet and shy voice that kept cracking, as if she hadn't spoken in a long time.

She said, "The king wont' be happy that you brought an unannounced guest."

Liam said, "We have a good reason for bringing her, Trista."

She said nothing else before starting to walk away. Kyra, Liam, and I followed closely behind her. I was too distracted looking at the artwork to notice I had fallen behind until I saw Liam turn a corner. I chased after them and caught up when they eventually stopped at a double door. That was when I noticed that Kyra was not there.

I turned to Liam and asked, "Where is Kyra?"

"She went to freshen up," he said.

Trista had opened the door slowly and quietly as if she was afraid of making a sound. When the door was opened, I was able to see the inside of the meeting room. The room's walls were white, and sections were covered with elaborate blue and white tapestry that had faded because of age. The floors were black marble. In the middle of the room was a huge wooden circular table with matching identical wooden chairs, except one. One of the chairs had a taller back that had three points at the top, somewhat resembling a crown. *That must be where the king sits*, I thought. Above the table was a large glass and metal black chandelier. Standing off to the side staring out the window, a tall man with dark hair turned and walked over toward us. He wore an expensive black suit with a short black cape that covered only his left side. He had beautiful black eyes and short black hair and tan skin.

He walked over to us and said, "Trista, my sweet little sister, why don't you go have a seat while Liam and I have a little talk."

Trista quickly made her way to the empty seat on the left side of the crowned chair.

The king said, "Hello, Liam. I hope you and Kyra's travel went well."

"Yes, our travels went extremely well. Thank you for asking, Your Highness. Kyra went to freshen up; she should be joining us shortly." Liam then grabbed my arm roughly and pulled me forward so I was no longer behind him. Liam said, "This is Bora from Arm. The reason we have brought her here to see you is because we are not sure what or who she is." Liam unraveled the bandages on my arm, revealing my fading scales.

"Why are you three having a discussion in the doorway?"

We all looked behind us to see Kyra standing there. Kyra was now wearing a dull blue dress with long sleeves that covered the scars on her arms. Her once messy mane of hair was now tamed and in a high ponytail. Then she curtsied and said, "Your Highness."

"Kyra, you're looking as lovely as always I see." He continued, "I believe you are right; this is not the best place to have this conversation." He turned to me, held out his hand, and said, "As you know, I am King Maverick, and I am pleased to meet you Bora from Arm."

I said, "I am honored to meet you, Your Highness."

He extended his hand, and I shook his strong warm hand.

King Maverick said, "Why don't you have a seat right next to Kyra!"

Kyra piped up and said, "That's perfect. Thank you."

We all headed to our seats. King Maverick took his usual seat at the head of the table, and Liam sat next to a woman with short black hair. The woman seemed to be out of sorts and had a blank expression on her face. She wore all black, similar to Trista, but instead of a dress, she wore a ruffled black blouse and black pants. She was sitting in her seat giggling to herself in an unsettling way. Next to Liam was where Kyra sat, and I took the seat on the other side of her.

King Maverick said, "Bora, let me introduce you to my second sister, Ann," while gesturing to the woman between him and Liam. "My sister Trista, I believe you two have already met. Sitting next to Trista is Theron, one of the oldest on the board of governors."

The man named Theron was wearing dated clothes. His hair was the color of straw. His eyes were a dull yellow color. He looked as if his mind was thousands of miles away, clearly uninterested in what was going on in the world around him. In his hand was a lit cigar that every once in a while he would bring to his lips and gently puff on it.

King Maverick said, "Theron, put out your cigar."

Theron's eyes shifted to King Maverick. He let out a huff in annoyance as he smashed the tip of his cigar into an oval copper ashtray.

King Maverick said, "Next to Theron is Willow, my top trusted advisor."

Willow was an old black woman who had drifted off to sleep before we had arrived. She looked to be in her late seventies or early eighties and was very wrinkled. She wore a dark green long-sleeved jumper. Her hair was short, gray, and with tight curls. Theron turned his attention to Willow and shook one of her shoulders, forcing her awake. Her light green eyes popped open, and it took her a moment to remember where she was.

The first thing she said was, "Forgive me, Your Highness. It appears I had fallen asleep." Willow seemed to be a kind and wise old woman but, despite these characteristics, always spoke her mind.

King Maverick said, "Everyone, this is Bora from Arm. Liam and Kyra have brought her here today to meet with us. It seems she has unexplained marks on her lower arm."

As he pointed to my scales, Theron did a painfully fake laugh and said, "Never knew you had a sense of humor, King Maverick. The odds that she is anything remarkable are very unlikely; she is most likely carrying a family curse."

Willow elbowed Theron in the side while saying, "Don't be rude, Theron."

"Does anyone want something to drink before the meeting begins?" King Maverick asked.

Ann just sat there and continued giggling and said, "I have a raw egg in a glass of milk."

"No," King Maverick said immediately.

Liam spoke up and said, "Kyra, Bora, and I will just have water."

"Very well," King Maverick said. "Willow, would you like some tea? I know how much you enjoy it."

"Yes. Thank you, Your Highness," Willow replied.

King Maverick continued to wear a soft smile on his face and said, "How about you, Theron? Would you like something to drink?"

Theron bluntly said, "Whiskey."

Before King Maverick could reply, Liam chimed in and asked, "Theron, can you really not stand being sober for one afternoon?"

Theron said, "Shut up, Liam. You should know better than to be so disrespectful. I may look young, but I am the oldest person in the room."

King Maverick said, "Trista, my dear little sister, can you go get some whiskey for Theron, some tea for Willow and me, and water for the rest?"

"What kind of tea?" Trista asked.

King Maverick was about to speak but then closed his mouth to think. King Maverick asked, "Willow, is there any specific tea you want?"

Willow hummed for a moment, thinking how to answer. She said, "Any tea is fine for me."

"Very well," he said. "Two cups of ginger tea."

"I believe we're out of ginger tea," Trista sheepishly said.

"Fine. Make it peppermint tea."

With that, Trista stood up and left the room.

I turned to Kyra and quietly asked, "Why isn't a maid or servant getting the drinks?"

Kyra whispered back, "There were a few poisonings in the past involving the royal families. So King Maverick refuses to let anyone other than himself and Trista to serve the food or drinks."

I nodded.

Eventually, the door creaked open as Trista returned with a silver tray full of drinks. Trista served the drinks to everyone. When it was my turn to get a drink, she stuffed a note in my hand under the table as she placed the water in front of me and walked away. Under the table, I unraveled the note and read. "Never drink."

King Maverick took a sip of his tea before saying, "With no other interruptions, let the meeting begin. First, I have a few questions for Bora. Liam has stated that you don't know who or what you are; is that correct?"

"Yes, sir," I said.

King Maverick continued, "Where is your family?"

I explained how I had woken in the forest not knowing who or where I was, how I found my way to the village of Arm and no one in the town seemed to know who I was either. I then traveled to Bateau where I met Kyra and Liam.

King Maverick nodded his head and then turned to Theron and said, "Theron, you are the governor of Arm. Have you ever seen Bora before?"

Theron looked at me and said, "Of course not. I don't personally associate with her kind."

King Maverick looked puzzled and said, "Very interesting. I hope you can find your family, Bora. If there is anything I can do to help, please let me know?

"Now, let's get down to business. I need the villages and countryside reports from the governors."

Theron and Kyra had a look of dread on their faces.

Willow started by saying, "Frosia had a late winter storm, so many of their crops were frozen over, but thankfully, Bartrex, Loup, and Westin are giving them food and some supplies." She paused and said, "Josay has been having a very bad flu outbreak, so most of my time has been spent trying to contain the sick."

King Maverick nodded and said, "Very good."

Liam spoke and said, "Bateau is thriving very well in fishing and trade. Along with Toujours and Avoir, there were a few sea serpent attacks, but they appeared to stop on their own."

Theron chuckled and said, "The attacks stopped because Bora sliced off part of its upper jaw. Isn't that right, Bora from Arm?"

Everyone but Theron looked at me surprised.

I replied, "Arm was burned to the ground in a Minotaur raid. My friends and I lost everything, and we moved to Bateau. We were on the ship heading to Bateau, and one day during a storm, a sea serpent attacked the ship. So I fought it. It just so happened to lose part of its jaw in the end." I turned to Theron and asked, "Theron, how did you know about the sea serpent?"

"Sometimes I just know," he said.

"A woman who is not afraid to fight—I respect that," King Maverick said.

In anger, I turned to Theron and said, "You are Arm's governor and guardian. Why didn't you do anything to stop the Minotaur raid? So many people lost their lives, and you had the nerve to just stand by and watch."

Theron curled his lips into a lazy smile and said, "The answer is easy." He continued, "As in the past, we are not allowed to intervene between humans and Minotaurs."

After a few seconds of silence King Maverick said, "Kyra, I would like to hear your report now?"

All the color from Kyra's tanned face vanished from these few words King Maverick had spoken. She took a deep breath and said, "Knox, Vex, and Espere have droughts going on. We could use your help, Your Majesty. Rain is really needed, and since that is your specialty, it would be greatly appreciated."

King Maverick huffed and said, "I will visit Knox, Vex, and Espere by the end of the week." He turned to Theron and said, "Theron, your report."

Theron just ignored him.

King Maverick inhaled deeply and exhaled and said, "Bora, you are from Arm. Tell me what it was like when you were there because Theron is ambiguous."

I paused before speaking and said, "Arm is now deserted. The town was burned to the ground during the Minotaur raid. Less than half of the townspeople had survived, and they all left for Bateau."

King Maverick nodded and said, "Well, the last thing we need to talk about is. . ."

But I didn't hear the rest of what he said. I suddenly noticed a black cat sitting in the corner of the room. He got up and stretched and walked around the perimeter of the room. He looked me dead in the eyes, then he stared at King Maverick before walking over to the door where it was slightly ajar. The door creaked as the cat opened it enough for it to squeeze through.

"Bora," someone said loudly.

I jumped as I refocused on the meeting. Kyra and Liam looked at me concerned. King Maverick was sipping his tea, and everyone else was getting ready to go. I felt embarrassed. *Of course, only I can space out during an important dragon meeting.* "Sorry. I got distracted by the cat."

King Maverick's eyes went wide, and he started choking on his tea. Ann looked at me as if I was crazy. Trista, Kyra, Liam, and Willow all looked confused, and last was Theron who didn't seem to care whatsoever.

King Maverick was stunned and asked, "What did the cat look like?"

I hesitated before answering, "Black fur, one green and one blue eye with a tear in its left ear."

King Maverick nodded and said, "Kyra and Ms. Bora, you are free to leave."

Kyra grabbed my arm and led me out of the room until we reached the middle of the corridor. She let go of me and continued to walk ahead at a fast pace. In the Great Hall was a line of portraits in golden frames. Eight large portraits were hung of the past and present rulers of Inue. Kyra pointed to each portrait, starting with the first ruler at the far end of the hall, and named each of the rulers in order.

She said, "The first portrait is Queen Phoenix, and next to her is Queen Zena and then King Theodore, King Arnold, King Frederick, King Lowel, Queen Sada, and last of course is King Maverick."

I could see that each portrait had a name plaque and a brief description of each ruler. I was drawn to the portrait of Queen Sada. She was the only one in the portraits who was smiling, and I understood why, because she had the sweetest smile I had ever seen. She had long blond hair and large brown eyes, and her beauty made her stand out from all the other portraits. She was wearing a royal blue dress with gold accents. A black cat was comfortably sitting on her lap. It appeared to be the same cat that I had seen over and over again. There was an inscription on the bottom of the frame, but before I could go over and read it I heard Kyra's voice.

"Come along, Bora."

I quickly ran down the corridor until I caught up to her. We walked out of the palace doors, and Kyra said, "It's a beautiful day. Let's take a walk in the garden while we wait for Liam."

Kyra and I strolled through the garden taking in all the beautiful of the white and black flowers.

Kyra said, "It's not hard to figure out that King Maverick is obsessed with strategies and chess. I have heard he is a very cunning opponent and almost always wins."

She continued, "I have a confession to make to you, Bora. Remember when I found you in the library at Vor Langer? I didn't accidentally spot you in the Mammoth Forest. I had been following you for weeks, ever since the fight in the square in Bateau. That night after we fought in the square, Liam and I talked, and we were curious about who or what you are. So we decided that I, having more time, would follow you to get some answers."

I turned to Kyra and thanked her for being honest with me. I asked her if she was able to find out anything about my past.

She slowly shook her head and said, "No."

Not long after, Liam came out into the garden. Kyra went back to the palace and changed into comfortable travel clothes. Liam shifted into his dragon form, and Kyra and I climbed on Liam's back, and as he took off and flew away, I looked back one last time. I had a feeling this would not be the last time I'd be at the castle.

CHAPTER 6

Anyone Home

AFTER WE LEFT THE CASTLE, I asked Kyra, with a little shame in my voice, "So what did I miss when I spaced out at the meeting?"

Kyra shrugged and said, "Not much. We talked about where the Phoenix Festival would be held."

"The what?" I asked.

Kyra looked at me. She pinched the bridge of her nose and said, "Of course, you can't remember anything from the past. Basically, whichever governor takes the best care of their lands gets to host the Phoenix Festival. This year Liam is the one who gets to host it in Bateau. The Phoenix Festival is held in honor of Queen Phoenix, our first ruler. It is just a big party with food, dancing for the people of Inue."

"Sounds wonderful. How often do you and the other dragons meet, and are there any more of you?"

Kyra said, "King Maverick assigned the territories, and we check in every three months and report on our food supplies, crime, and the general well-being of the territories and its people. It is believed that there may be other half-breed dragons who are still in hiding and have chosen not to reveal themselves."

I looked at her and asked, "Don't you live in Bateau with Liam?"

Kyra didn't look at me but said, "My lands or territories are some of the hottest and driest of this world. That's a problem for most dragons because their scales dry out, which causes them to bleed, and it also creates other skin conditions. But I am a fire dragon, and my ancestors used to live near volcanoes. I don't live there because it is too dry like a tinderbox. The townspeople are terrified because of my fire abilities. They fear their towns will burn down. So I don't spend much time there. Also, Liam and I have been together a very, very long time. It would look weird if we weren't together."

I felt somewhat bad for her not to be wanted by people in her own territory. Now that I thought about it, Bateau treated Liam like a king, and poor Kyra wasn't even wanted back in her territory. I gave her a tight hug and patted her on the back as we flew home, or the place we all called our home by choice or for convenience. The image of Queen Sada from the portrait was still in my mind.

I spoke carefully and asked, "How did Queen Sada die?"

She spoke softly, which was odd considering her naturally booming voice, "Queen Sada was hard working and a people pleaser, which caused a lot of people to take advantage of her." She stopped speaking and closed her eyes tightly as if it was difficult to remember. She began to speak again.

"Neither Liam nor I knew her very well. I heard that she had really wanted a child. There are a lot of rumors about how she died. The official report said that her baby died during childbirth. Her husband and father of the child had gone missing prior to the birth, and in her grief, she took her own life."

"What do you mean she took her own life?" I said.

Kyra was quiet, but Liam chimed in with a growl-like voice and said, "She jumped in a river and drowned."

"I have one more question if it is alright to ask," I said.

Kyra said, "Go for it."

"Why are you so unsure if I'm a dragon or rather a dragoness?"

Kyra said matter-of-factly, "We don't know who your parents were or whether your mom was a dragoness."

"Why do you phrase it like that?" I asked.

She replied, "Only a dragoness can pass on the dragon gene. She could be a dragoness in hiding. So we don't know if you are one of us or something else entirely."

"How do you know I'm not one of the other dragoness's children?"

Kyra said, with a cocky grin, "It is an easy process of elimination. You look to be around eighteen, but you may just be short.

Willow is far too old to have children. Ann is just a no, considering most, if not all, men fear her. Even Liam is afraid of Ann."

"Really?" I said.

"Yes, big time," Kyra said, again smiling, while Liam let out a growl of disapproval.

Kyra continued, "There is Trista, and considering her tortured past and her mistrust of humans, it is safe to assume she is out of the picture. Then there is me," she chuckled and said. "Liam is not the kind to have a child out of wedlock."

I said back to her jokingly, "I don't know; why don't you tell me about it, Mom?"

This caused Kyra to start laughing harder while Liam let out a huff of disapproval, not thinking my joke was very funny.

Since we got a late start at sunset, we landed in a clearing in the woods. Liam changed back into his human form and started to bark orders. I was in charge of setting up an area to sleep, Kyra was in charge of the fire, and Liam was in charge of food. At night, Kyra took the first watch, and later Liam sat up leaning against a tree with his eyes half closed. I awoke to hearing Liam walking away. Suddenly, Liam started to walk quickly toward the woods.

"Liam, where are you going?" Kyra asked.

Liam kept up his speed and said, "I am going to get some more firewood."

Kyra looked at me and pointed at the fairly good-sized pile of firewood nearby as we waited for Liam to come back. "Liam has good instincts," Kyra said, as we wondered what Liam might have heard. After some time, Liam came back to the campsite carrying a sword.

"What is going on?" Kyra asked.

Liam quietly sat down and said, "I had the feeling we were being watched, so I went to check it out. I snuck up on a man and asked him if there was a problem. The man pulled out a knife and said, 'Give me all your possessions.' I just stood there, thinking this was some kind of joke. I said, 'Yeah, I don't think so.

"As soon as I said that, a second man jumped down from a tree. He had a sword in hand, and with one quick movement, he tried to slice me. I caught his arm holding the sword and twisted it until he heard it snap. The man let out a scream and took off running. The other man with the knife then apologized.

"I told him to get lost and then next time he won't be so lucky. Kyra, here, I got you a new sword," Liam said and handed the sword to Kyra.

She held it up straight in front of her toward the sky. "The end bends slightly to the right. This is not a well-made sword," she said.

Liam smiled slightly and said, "We both know you enjoy black-smithing and you are quite good at it."

"Flattery is not an excuse, Liam. You should have told me. I would have enjoyed watching them squirm."

"No offense to you, Kyra, but I did not want to see the entire forest burn down."

That was the last thing I heard before closing my eyes and falling asleep.

As soon as we were back to Bateau, I thanked both Kyra and Liam for bringing me along with them before running home to see Nessa, Kat, and the others. When I arrived, Amos was holding Kat and trying unsuccessfully to calm her down. It looked like Nessa was teaching Avery how to make some of her herbal medicines. I noticed Amos had his hand wrapped in a bandage.

"I'm gone for a couple of days, and this is what I come home to," I said.

Nessa, Amos, and Avery all jumped in surprise, and Kat stopped crying and started smiling and laughing because she thought it was funny seeing everyone jump. Avery was the first to start talking.

She said, "Amos was cutting wood with a dull axe. It bounced; he lost his grip and he caught it by the blade and the blade cut his hand."

Avery continued, "I am helping Nessa make up for lost time because someone around here is always in need of mending."

I could not believe how much I had missed them all and happily listened to accounts of what I had missed in my absence. I sat next to Nessa, and Avery held Kat on my lap and helped them produce the rest of their medicine. I was happy to be home.

A week after arriving home, I received a letter with a royal seal. The letter was from King Maverick who was asking for a favor. The letter stated that Theron was in possession of an historic journal and was refusing to return it, and because Theron seemed to have taken an interest in me, maybe I could ask Theron to borrow the journal. King Maverick said that he had heard about the incident in the library from Kyra and he was willing to pay me double the money that the hag had promised me. He said he would pay me either way whether Theron gave me the journal or not. I knew that I had to take this job, and it seemed like easy money. Nessa was willing to let me go, but Avery was not happy about it one bit. She kept saying it could be another trap and questioned if King Maverick could be trusted.

Against her wishes, I bought a ticket to travel the next day on a ship going to Arm leaving in the early evening. I was going by boat to avoid upsetting Theron with the presence of Kyra or Liam. That day seemed to go by quickly. I told my boss again that I had personal business to take care of and would again have to miss a few weeks of work. He said that he hoped this would be the last time, and if not, he was going to have to replace me. I spent some time holding and playing with Kat. The hardest part was when I looked at Avery and Amos and I could see the fear in their eyes. Before I knew it, evening came, and the ship would soon set sail. I said my goodbyes and left.

After I boarded the ship, I saw a cloaked figure running toward the dock and jumping onto the stern of the boat. The cloaked figure turned toward me, taking off the hood of their cloak, and I saw that it was Avery standing there. She gave me a frustrated look as my eyes purposely avoided hers.

The first mate walked over to her and said, "Lady, you need a ticket to board this ship. It is beyond capacity."

Avery glared at him and pushed two gold coins into his hand. Avery then said, "Is this enough, or do I need to throw someone off?"

The first mate stood there wide-eyed and said, "I stand corrected. There is enough room on the ship for you."

"Good. That's what I thought," she said. Then she walked away.

The first mate and I stared at her until she was out of sight. I had forgotten how intimidating she could be. I, of course, apologized to the first mate for her behavior. Avery and I shared a small bed. I decided that the next morning I would try and fix things with her, but when I awoke, she was gone and already on the upper deck.

I walked up on the deck looking for Avery who I noticed was staring at what looked like the never-ending ocean in front of us. I quietly approached her and stood next to her. We didn't say a word. We just looked at the horizon.

Avery sighed and finally said, "I don't get you."

I looked at her and said, "What do you mean?"

She spoke with her voice shaking with anger, "You are willing to put yourself in danger. You risk your life for strangers you don't even know. You have too much faith in people. You've seen what a hellhole this life is, how horrible people treat each other. How can you still be so nice and good after all this?"

I stayed quiet and thought momentarily. She was not wrong; this world we lived in was cruel and dangerous. I eventually said, "The world is only the way you make it out to be. If you only focus on the bad things, then you'll be too blind to see all the good in it. The world is not dangerous because of all the bad people in it, but it is dangerous because of the people who witness the bad and still do nothing."

She stared at me, speechless, before saying, "When did you get so wise, Bora?" as a small smile made its way to her lips.

I reflected on our first meeting. How funny this was: It was just months ago when I met this young woman. She actually hated me, and now she was willing to risk her life for me.

Three days later, with a strong tailwind, we arrived at Arm. We walked through where the town used to be. Most of the buildings had been burnt down, and all that was left was the charred remains. Nature had started to take over, and the graves I had dug were barely visible. We kept walking until we reached the willow tree I had woken up under and stopped. We rested there for a moment. Avery got distracted looking for her canteen. After a few moments of silence, I started a conversation.

I asked Avery, "What did you and Amos do for work before we met?"

Avery's smile disappeared, and she was quiet for a moment, contemplating how to answer. Then a smile made its way back to her lips as she said, "How about this? When you remember your past and tell me about it, I will tell you about Amos's and my past. Does that sound fair?"

"Sounds fair," I chuckled, and then said, "Fair enough."

Shortly thereafter, the black cat appeared from behind a tree and looked me dead in the eyes. It then ran away. I followed him, and Avery followed close behind me.

"Do you even know where you're going?" she yelled from behind me.

I smiled and yelled back, "Nope."

The cat led us to an old burnt-down cottage with a large over-grown garden. I took a closer look. It all seemed familiar to me. There was a mysterious sound of music dancing in the wind. It was a slow melancholy tone. We followed where the noise was coming from, and it led us to a two-story house that was bigger than any of the remaining homes in Arm. It was red brick, and all the nearby plants were overgrown, giving it the illusion of being abandoned. A window was open, and lights were on the second floor. Avery knocked on the door, but the music was so loud that whoever was in there didn't hear us. She kept knocking, louder and louder each time. I quietly snuck away and climbed a tree. My plan was to climb the tree to get in from the open window. But there was one small problem: all the branches at the top were too skinny or were cut back. I took a deep breath and jumped like a frog, trying to land near the window ledge. I landed on the roof right under the window. I barely made it onto the edge of the roof, landing with a big thud, causing Avery to look up.

Her eyes widened, looking as if they were going to pop out of her head as she yelled, "Are you crazy? What are you doing?"

I crouched, trying to find my balance. I used all the strength I had, pulled myself up, and climbed in the window. I took a moment to catch my breath and sat on the floor. The room was dark, but after a few minutes, my eyes adjusted. It seemed like I was in a study or an office. Theron sat at a piano with a full glass of whiskey.

He stopped playing and said, "Dragons—they call us, yet we are just the false half breed they failed to exterminate, unlike the real ones."

After a moment, I heard him mumble in a sad melancholic voice. He said, "She is gone." He shut his eyes tightly and gripped his side as if he was in too much pain to keep his eyes open.

In the room, all the furniture was covered in white sheets, all except for the piano and two items in a corner. There was a portrait of a very beautiful woman with pearl white hair and eyes similar to Liam's. She had a soft smile, and I could tell from the look in her eyes that she was a kind woman. Beneath the portrait was a violin case leaning against the wall. Seconds later, I heard someone screaming my name. That was when Theron noticed my presence in the room. I turned my attention back out the window and saw Avery looking worried.

I shouted back at her, "I'm ok."

Theron then turned to me and said, "How can you handle being around humans all the time?"

"Humans are not so bad," I said.

"Humans are evil." He turned and said, "Do you want to hear a joke?"

I hesitated and nodded slowly.

He said, "They call themselves humans, but they're just inhumane."

He chuckled, but I could tell from his voice that a broken heart was behind it, and I felt sorry for him. I truly did. He then sat straight up on the piano bench, his eyes narrowed behind me. I turned my head to see what had gotten his attention and then back to him. I asked him if there was something wrong.

He said, "Nothing. Nothing at all. Just my old eyes playing tricks on me."

I looked along the bare walls and saw on a shelf there was an old photo with a group of young adults and children. On the right side was the girl from the portrait with the pearl hair, but there was a glare from the sunlight that distorted her face at that moment the picture was taken. Next to her in the picture was Theron. He was much older now, but I would guess that he should have looked much older than how he looked today.

So I asked him, "Theron, aren't you older than Willow? Because you don't look it."

His face hardened before answering, "I was cursed a long time ago, even though we dragons age much slower than humans. I have barely aged in the last 250 years. I should happily be at the end of my life by now. My life and memories continue to go on."

He was much younger and healthier in the picture than he looked today, like he had been eating proper meals and, obviously, he did not have a drinking problem in his younger years. Below the girl with the pearl hair was a young dark-skinned boy in worn-out clothing, and he was missing part of his left arm above his elbow. He had the widest smile on his face I had ever seen. Next to him was a little girl. She was in front of Theron. She looked younger than the boy but not by much. She wore a green oversized shirt as a dress, and her dark black hair was in pigtails. Her smile was not as big because she was missing her two front teeth. On the right side of the picture were burn marks that looked as if the picture had been burned to erase someone from the picture. A hand and part of an arm could be seen around Theron's shoulder, but the person's face and body had been burnt away. Theron stood up, walked over to me, and tipped the picture over so the photo was now hidden. On the back of the photo were the names of the people: Willow, Oak, Pricilla, Theron, and Bonnie. Theron then walked back to his piano stool and plopped himself down on it.

Theron said, "You know it is rude to enter someone's residence without being invited in, don't you, girly?" While staring at me, he said, "I presume Maverick sent you here for the journal. Is that true?"

I slowly nodded, watching him stand up and leave the room. After a moment, he came back with the journal in hand and held it out to me. It looked old and tattered and had a dark green leather cover.

I looked at him and said, "Why are you giving this to me if you don't want Maverick to have it?"

He winced and said, "I believe this was left here for you. You should have it. And you can decide what you want to do with it."

I looked at him wide-eyed and said, "Who left this for me? Is this a clue to who I am?"

"You will have to wait until it can be opened because you can't read it now," he said.

"I can't open it; why not?" I asked.

"It has a spell on it. Trust me; I've tried to open it in the past, but all the pages are stuck together except the front and back cover," he said.

He then grabbed his side and winced in pain before guzzling down the rest of his whiskey. He then headed downstairs. Each step he took creaked as if at any moment the stairs would give out.

I quickly followed him and said, "How do you break the spell?"

He walked past several rooms, which were bare with little to no furniture, and those that did have furniture were covered with white sheets. He pushed a door open. I continued to follow him. The room he had entered now was the kitchen. It looked as deserted as the rest of the house; there wasn't even a stove.

"How do I break the spell, Theron?" I said loudly as he rummaged through the empty pantry.

"To break it, you'll need some pretty powerful magic and, unfortunately, King Maverick may be the only option for you."

Theron started to go down the list of other dragons. "My magic doesn't work on the spell. Kyra would burn the book to ashes. Liam would ruin it with water. Willow studied magic, so she may have been able to do it in her prime, but now she is too weak. Trista has lost her ability to control magic unless it is very simple, while Ann is so deranged that she can't be trusted. I doubt you can find a witch powerful enough to do it. And then there is you, and you can't do magic, can you, Dora?"

"It's Bora," I snapped back.

"Whatever," he said. "It looks like I'm out anyway," he said.

I looked at Theron as he stepped out of the pantry and closed the door behind him. Theron then said, "Everything—I'm out of everything, it appears."

He walked out of the kitchen toward the front door. The door had been boarded up for a very long time, given how rusty the nails were. By the door was an old coat rack that was well used, and that was putting it lightly, by the shape it was in. The coat rack went well with the worn-out, abandoned character of the house. Off the coat rack, Theron pulled a worn-out brown leather jacket before walking up the creaky stairs. I followed closely behind him. We were halfway up the stairs when one of the stairs gave out, causing my left leg to fall through the wooden step. Luckily my other foot was on the step above it; if not, I would have fallen through. Theron glanced over his shoulder at me. We locked eyes uncomfortably for a moment. He then turned his head forward as he continued to climb the stairs. It took some effort to pull my leg out of the hole in the stairs, and I hissed in pain as I did so. Once it was out, I examined my leg and noticed there was a large bleeding gash that ran halfway along my calf to my foot. In my ankle, there were several large wood splinters. I hobbled up the stairs and searched for Theron.

When I finally found him, he was in the same room as before, with the piano. I limped over to the piano bench, which was the only seat in the room, and plopped myself down.

Theron said, "It took you long enough," his voice not revealing a bit of empathy for me.

I turned to him and asked, "Do you have any disinfectant or vodka?"

Theron faked an offended gasp and said, "How dare you? This is a 'whiskey only' house, young lady!"

My right hand was pressed tightly on my leg, applying pressure to the cut, but a puddle of blood was starting to form on the floor around my foot. I said, "Do you have any centella asiatica, curcuma longa, or aloe vera? I am going to need a disinfectant."

"No, I don't have any of that, but I do have my charming good looks."

I gritted my teeth and said, "Not funny, Theron. I am losing a lot of blood and it's going to get an infection. How about soap and water?"

He gave me an irritated scowl and said, "Ok, the sooner your leg is mended the sooner you'll leave, right? And then we can get this over with. You need to pull those splinters out of your ankle and I will do the rest."

I nodded and removed the wood splinters out of my ankle. He pulled a gold pocket watch out of his pocket, but his hand was cradling it, so I was unable to get a good look at the watch. He stared intensely at the gold pocket watch and his gold eyes were motionless. My leg started to feel hot, and a couple of minutes later I saw my open wound starting to close. It began to heal, a scab formed, and the broken skin tissue was growing back together. I looked at my leg and the cut was completely gone now, not even leaving behind a scar.

"What happened? How? Is that gold watch magic?" I asked.

Theron said, "No, it is not magic. I just use it as a tool to help me harness my powers. I don't really need it, but it gives me something to concentrate on."

"How does it work?" I asked.

Theron ignored my question and said, "Stop your lollygagging. It's time to leave."

Without saying another word, Theron climbed out of the open window. I got up off the piano stool, grabbed the journal, and stuck it in the waistband of my pants. Theron then jumped to the ground below. I climbed out the window, hung by my arms, and hit the ground hard on my feet. I was thankful Theron had healed my leg. It would have been impossible to land otherwise. Avery was waiting on the ground, sitting with her back leaning against the tree.

I showed Avery the journal and told her, "The journal was left here for me, but it is cursed and I am unable to open it." I turned to Theron and asked again who had left it for me.

"All in due time" was all he said.

Avery said, "Is this the famous Theron? I am surprised. You seem completely sober."

For a second, I thought I saw a smile curl his lips before saying, "Good to see my reputation precede me. Come on; I'll fly you to the castle to drop off your journal. First, we will make a stop in Bateau and drop off your little friend. Maverick doesn't like unexpected guests. I have to get some supplies in town anyways."

I thought to myself that the first thing on his supply list was probably his whiskey.

Avery said, "Is it safe with your reputation?"

Theron chuckled and said, "Let me explain. First is that you already have flown with Kyra who lets her emotions cloud her judgment. Second is that it's faster and I'm going there anyway, so we're practically killing two humans with one bolder."

Before Theron could finish, Avery said, "Don't you mean two birds with one stone?"

Theron said, "No, I like my way better, and shoosh—it is rude to talk over someone when they are talking." He continued speaking, "The third is because I have had very little to drink today. I ran out hours ago, and because I am the only one able to take you at the moment. . ."

"Ok, I get it" I said.

But Theron continued, "Well, the lovebirds are busy out on a trip together or something."

"By lovebirds you mean Liam and Kyra?" I said.

Theron said, "Well, look at that. You might actually have a brain in that mostly empty head of yours. Now why can't Trista or Ann fly you?" Theron asked.

"Because they both live at the castle," I replied.

Theron said sarcastically, "Very good. And why can't you go with Willow?"

I hesitated, not answering, not knowing where all the towns and villages were that Willow was the governor of.

Theron said in an irritated voice, "I take back everything I just said about you. From where we are currently, you would actually have to walk past the castle to get to her. If you both continue to complain, I think I'll take back my offer to fly you."

Avery stopped arguing with him, begrudgingly. Theron walked back a few steps. Within seconds, where Theron once stood was a long, large, thin dragon. He was far longer than Liam or Kyra; his length was almost double their size. His scales were a dark golden brown. On his head was a golden V shape that started at the crown of his head and went down between his eyes. He had two long golden horns on each side of his head. Out of all the dragons I had seen thus far, he was the most beautiful and mystifying. Though at what cost? His body was missing scales in several places and instead were scars that had healed long ago, so many you couldn't count them. The scars and missing scales now revealed his rosy pink flesh underneath. His eyes were a brilliant gold color, unlike the pale gold of his human form. Theron's eyes were the most wild and beautiful of all. His eyes were more primal of someone who had lost everything and he bore the weight of that loss alone. Avery and I stared at him.

Theron snapped and said, "Any time, ladies. We don't have all day."

With that, Avery and I climbed on his back, and we took off into the sky. Theron was far slower than the other dragons. I wondered if it was due to his age. As we flew, I allowed the breeze to clear my mind, and I looked down at the old journal in my hands. I traced my hands over the old cover, memorizing the feel of the soft leather.

I hesitated a moment before opening it. When I tried to look at the rest of the pages, they were all stuck together. I kept trying to pry them apart, but Avery put her hand over mine and said, "You will have to wait until the spell is lifted."

"I know," I said. "But this was left behind for me."

Even though I was frustrated, I smiled, knowing that this journal could hold all the answers to my past. My past seemed to be closer than ever. After two days of traveling, we dropped Avery off in Bateau and then headed for the castle.

Once we reached the castle, Theron then shifted back into his human form and said, "I have things to do. I will see you later. If you're not here by the time I get back, I'm leaving without you," and he walked away and headed down to the city below.

I knocked on the door of the castle, and it was slowly opened by a maid. She was a little taller than me with soft strawberry-blonde hair and fresh scratch marks on her arms.

The maid asked, "What is your purpose?"

I replied, "King Maverick invited me here."

"Do you have any proof?" she asked, now glaring at me.

"Oh no, I don't have the letter with me. May I have your name?" I asked in a cold voice.

She said, "Why would you want to know that?"

"So I can tell His Majesty King Maverick why I am late, because he cleared his extremely busy schedule for our meeting, and when he finds out that you are the reason I didn't show up, he'll be mad and you will have to pay the consequences," I said.

The maid looked at me with sheer terror. I felt my stomach drop when I saw her expression.

The maid said, "Very well. Please come in and give me your name?"

"My name is Bora from Arm," I said.

"Stay here while I inform King Maverick of your arrival."

I stood for a moment, but I needed to know what was written on the bottom of the portrait of Queen Sada, the woman with the golden hair. So I quickly and quietly made my way down the hallway. As I got closer, I wanted to stop and study all the portraits and read the placards placed under them, but right now I had to know what the portrait had said. Once I reached the portrait, I closed my eyes, took a deep breath, and hoped that my heart rate would abate. The placard read "*Queen Sada was wise, brave, and strong and loved by her citizens. She was loved by everyone, but a broken heart led to her demise.*" I looked at the inscription again and again, hoping I missed something, but unfortunately, I hadn't.

"It was a shame for what fate fell upon her," a voice said behind me.

I jumped and turned my head and saw King Maverick standing next to me. I turned my attention back to the portrait. He paused and said, "I loved her very much, but alas, she and the child perished the night it was born. Not only was she grieving the death of her child, but her husband had abandoned her just days before."

I handed him the journal and said, "I hope you enjoy it," before walking away.

"Bora, you came such a long way. At least have a cup of tea with me," he said.

"I'm not sure—" I said.

But King Maverick quickly cut me off and said, "I insist."

As soon as he said that, I knew there was no point in arguing anymore. He led me to a living room area on the first floor. The room was large and open. All the furniture was very old but well cared for. I sat down on an old wooden black chair that was hard and worn smooth from years of use. The only color in the room was a big painting bordered with a golden frame. The painting showed a young girl who was dressed in a dark blue long-sleeved robe. She wore a ring of white flowers, like a crown covering her black hair. On each leg, she wore a single golden anklet, and she stood on a cold stone walkway. Her dark skin matched her brown eyes. The background was dark as if it were night, and it appeared she was standing in front of a brick wall. In her right hand, lifted above her head, she was holding a golden lantern, the only light in the painting. In her left hand, there was a matching blue fan that she held up to cover her mouth. The girl seemed extremely familiar to me, but the harder I thought about it, the more my head started to hurt. King Maverick turned around and saw what I was looking at.

He said, "Oh, you are admiring that old painting."

I stood and walked over to the painting to get a better look and stood in front of it. "Yes, if you don't mind me asking, who is the girl in the painting?"

King Maverick smiled and said, "The girl was a close and personal friend. Her name was Joy. She was orphaned when she was young and had no other family. Sada and her became inseparable; you rarely saw one without the other. After Sada's death, Joy became a nomad and I completely lost touch with her. Unfortunately, I heard she passed away not too long ago in a fire. She was a kind and strong woman who passed before her time."

I went and sat back down in the black chair that I had previously left.

Then King Maverick said, "Excuse me while I go get the tea."

I sat in the chair trying to get comfortable when I noticed something gray on the black carpet. I knelt down and touched it. It felt similar to sand and had a smoky smell. It was a large pile of ashes on the carpet.

"Bora, what are you doing?" King Maverick said.

I turned around and saw King Maverick with a tray in hand. I stood up and sat back down in the chair.

"I believe you have a pile of ashes on your carpet," I said.

King Maverick's once hard blank expression slowly melted away into a soft smile as he looked at me.

"What is it? I asked curiously.

But he just continued smiling and said,   "You have the prettiest eyes." Then King Maverick said angrily, "Dammit, Theron. I haven't used this room since he was last here, and obviously, the maids are not doing their job. I told Theron not to smoke on the carpet; the ash stains it, and the smell is impossible to get out." King Maverick saw that I still had some black ashy residue on my hands and said, "The restroom is down the hall on the left."

I thanked him before heading to the restroom.

After I had freshened up, I left quietly, closing the door behind me. I heard mumbling from around the corner. Trista stood there with her hair more matted than before, and her dress sleeves looked like they were clawed at by an animal. She mumbled something that I couldn't understand.

"I am sorry, are you talking to me?" I asked.

Her eyes looked directly into mine; they were no longer zigzagging around the corridor. Her hands flew up, gripping the top of my arms tightly. She said, "Never drink." She was finally speaking clearly.

"What do you mean by 'never drink'?" I asked.

She started pushing me into the wall while continuing to say, "Never drink."

By now, her very short nails were cutting into my arms as I tried to push her away. I was worried that this once sane woman whom I had met at the meeting was now nothing more than a crazy shell of her past self. I heard footsteps quickly approaching from around the corner. King Maverick appeared. He spoke in a calm voice, stepping forward slowly.

He said, "It's ok; it's ok. I'm right here. Let go of Bora."

Trista's nails dug more deeply into my skin causing me to flinch.

"Please, sister, let go of her," he said.

Trista loosened her grip, and her hands slowly slid off my arms as she hugged herself tightly and began shaking frantically. She said, "There were three. By the time next year is done, there will only be one."

King Maverick stared at Trista with sad eyes as she started laughing madly while clawing at his clothes. King Maverick yelled,

"Guards," as two men in uniforms came running down the corridor. King Maverick then said, "Take her to her room and keep her there."

We watched as the two guards dragged her off as she struggled to get away.

"Thank you, King Maverick. I don't know why she attacked me," I said.

I was still uneasy about what had happened. We headed back to the living room and returned to our seats, and King Maverick poured the tea from a white teapot with a gray dragon crescent on the sides into matching white teacups. He filled the cups almost to the brim. The tea had a sharp pungent gingery aroma, and the steam carried it throughout the room.

"Do you take lemon or cream with your tea?" he asked.

I just shook my head no.

He smiled and took a sip of the tea and said, "I'm sorry you had to see Trista like that."

I picked up the teacup and asked, "Do you mind me asking what happened to Trista?"

King Maverick took a deep breath and said, "Shortly before the War Against Dragons ended, my sisters and I were revealed as dragons. When people found out, they locked us up and tortured us for information, if we knew, about the location of any others of our kind." King Maverick paused and rolled up one of his sleeves, revealing his arm covered in scars. "When we were tortured, I was lucky that mine was only physical. My sisters were given drinks that poisoned their minds, causing them to descend into madness. Ann got the worst of it and is known to have violent outbursts quite frequently, while Trista seemed to be unfazed at first, but over the years, she has been getting increasingly worse. They take medication, but it doesn't always work. What you just saw in the corridor with Trista happens when the medication she is on has lost its effectiveness."

I looked down at my tea and placed it back on the tray without saying another word. King Maverick asked, "Don't you like the tea?" He then took another sip of his tea and sighed in satisfaction. King Maverick had a small yet joy-filled smile on his face when he said, "I love ginger tea."

"Really? Why ginger tea?" I asked curiously.

King Maverick said, "Being king is a very stressful job. It helps with headache and stomach issues. Being king is a task that is more difficult than I would like to admit. Now, as for your travels, were they well, my dear?"

"Yes, Your Highness, they were," I replied simply.

King Maverick nodded and said, "That is very good to hear. I was surprised to see you with Theron. He seems to tolerate you, unlike other humans. After all, he really doesn't seem to like anyone except Willow."

"I have a question, King Maverick, if you don't mind," I said.

"Go ahead. You may ask your question," he said.

"During the meeting, Theron stated that he was the eldest in the room, but he looks much younger than Ms. Willow. When I asked him about it, he told me he was cursed. And when I asked him who cursed him, he wouldn't tell me. Do you know who cursed Theron?"

King Maverick said, "That is a fairly complicated question to answer. We dragons age much slower than humans. Well, more precisely, the older we get, the slower we age. We normally slow down aging between the ages of twenty or thirty, and every couple of years, we age just a bit more. A dragon usually lives between two and three hundred years old. Theron, on the other hand, is a special case. Do you know what the War Against Dragon was?"

"Yes, that is when the extinction of the half-breed dragons started?"

King Maverick nodded his head in agreement and continued. "Shortly before the War Against Dragons started, all the true dragons were slayed by men. This was actually an easy feat for them, since the true dragons lived a solitary life. The War Against Dragons started because of men believing that the half-breed dragons were a dark force and blamed us for anything that went wrong in this world. We became the problem that needed to be fixed. A man named Arnold the Conqueror killed King Theodore while he was on his deathbed. This is important because King Theodore was sympathetic to the half breeds and had given many of them high ranking positions in the government. After King Theodore's death, Arnold was crowned king. He declared a manhunt for all the half breeds to be captured and killed in an arena for men's amusement. We believe Theron is cursed because he tried to use his powers in the area, but they didn't work and he managed to kill every living thing in that coliseum."

I saw how tightly King Maverick clenched his fist before taking a deep breath and letting it go.

I said, "Everyone has a hard time letting go of their suffering, whether it is because of the fear of not knowing how to move past it or because they prefer to hold on to what is familiar to them."

King Maverick said, "You know I think you're right about that, Bora."

"I have one final question to ask of you, King Maverick."

He looked at me puzzled and said, "Sure. My next meeting doesn't start for a while. I have some time, so ask your question!"

"Why does that journal mean so much to you?" I asked.

King Maverick stayed quiet for a moment before saying, "The journal is a historical account that was written by someone I cared about. It really belongs here at the castle and should be kept in the room of treasure. I wanted to read the journal because I want to see the world through their perspective before it all came crashing down."

I asked, "Who wrote the journal?"

"I am sorry, but I can't tell you that information because at this time it is considered classified. Once the journal is open and unclassified we will have to see."

I said, "Theron told me that you are the only person who may be able to unlock the journal. I am very interested in historical accounts from the past since I know nothing of my own, and I would love to read it once it has been unclassified."

"That's enough. Unfortunately, we have run out of time, Bora," King Maverick said, picking up the journal, standing up, and walking away. "You can see yourself out, can't you? There is a bag of coins waiting for you on your way out. Well, til we meet again, Bora. I have enjoyed our little talk," King Maverick said, before leaving the room.

I sat there for a minute or two before leaving. At the door stood a courtier holding a bag of coins, which he handed to me before I walked out of the door. I waited outside. Theron was nowhere to be seen. I decided to walk into town to look for him. The town was quiet. The people that lived here were in no hurry. They were among the well-to-do who didn't have to hustle to make a living. The town of Perth near the castle was full of rich people and important diplomats. The products for sale in the shops were only of the best quality and were very expensive. There were no children running wild or playing outside unsupervised. The buildings were well built and had elaborate architectural details. It did not take me long to find Theron. He was on his way back to the castle holding a lit cigar in his mouth and carrying a crate under his left arm.

On the ride home, I was happy that I had seen King Maverick again and learned more about him. I was also sad that I no longer had the journal in my possession and worried that I may never get the answers that hours earlier seemed so close.

CHAPTER 7

The Phoenix Festival

WHEN WE LANDED AT BATEAU, I was in a hurry to say our goodbyes. The Phoenix Festival was later that night, and I was excited to be going. Theron had landed in an open area near the inn. As soon as I hopped off his back, he shifted back into his human form.

He said to me, "I need to speak with you for a minute."

"We can speak tonight at the Phoenix Festival. I really need to get home and get ready," I said.

Theron said, "Please. I have something I want to tell you in private." Theron spoke in a voice that crackled with pain as he grabbed his side tightly. The one word he said that caught me off guard and made me a little concerned was "please." "Everything will get destroyed by someone or something whether it is by time, a creature/human, or even yourself. Now what will destroy you, girl?" he said.

"What do you mean by destroy?" I said.

Theron took out a cigar and lit it. He brought it up to his lips and inhaled. He lowered the cigar, puffing out a smoke ring. By now, I was very irritated having to wait for his answer.

Theron took notice of this and said, "Destroying can be interpreted in many different ways, but the most common one is self-destruction." He then stopped speaking, bringing his cigar back to his lips, and inhaled before again making a smoke ring.

At this point, I was losing my patience and said, "If we can finish our talk prior to when the festival is starting, that would be great." Theron seemed a little aggravated and said, "I'm trying to give you some advice, and you can't even give me a moment to think of the right words to say. Impatient, aren't you?"

Now I felt a little guilty and kept quiet.

Theron was quiet for another moment and then said, "Think of it like how a child changes one's life when she comes into the world, like that baby of yours. What is her name again? Kat?"

I was surprised because I had never spoken to him about Kat. I didn't ever remember saying her name.

"How did you know about Kat?" I asked.

Theron chuckled and said, "I know everything; remember who you are speaking with. I know all, especially about you, Bora, and let's just say that you are flying too close to the sun on wax wings."

"What do you want me to do? And why won't you tell me what I need to know about myself?" I said.

"When the time is right, I will tell you all I know. For now, keep your head down and stay home," Theron said, annoyed.

He was about to take his cigar out of his mouth again but stopped, his eyes darting behind me again, like what happened at his house in Arm. Yet something changed in him for a moment. It was brief, but it was there. He bit down so hard on his cigar that I thought he bit through it completely. The way his eyes narrowed, the way he clenched his fist tight. . . I turned my head around to see what was behind me, but there was nothing there. I turned my attention back to Theron who was still glaring at something behind me. I hesitated for a moment but reached out my hand to put on his shoulder. He was taller than me, so it was not an easy task. Right when I placed my hand on his shoulder, he swatted it away. His heavy breathing returned to its normal shallow tempo.

"Don't ever touch me," he said, playing it off as if it was nothing while rubbing the back of his neck. He then stopped for a moment before saying, "You might want to start locking your doors and windows, Lora."

I replied without hesitation, "Again, my name is Bora, not Lora or Dora or any other of the many names people have been calling me. Also, I live in an inn, and of course, we lock our door at night."

Theron said, "Good. Just checking. The world is a dangerous place." He turned his back to me and walked away.

I ran after him and yelled, "Wait! I have something to ask you."

"What is it, girl? I thought you were in a hurry to attend the Phoenix Festival and get back to that little makeshift family of yours."

I said, "When are you going to tell me about who left the journal for me? Above all, I have the right to know who left the journal. Was it my mother? My father? Someone else in my family? How and why did you get the journal? Who gave it to you, or did you take it?"

The cigar was still in his mouth and a little more than half of it was gone. "Let's just say the journal was given to me for safekeeping. I have nothing to tell you. One last thing—I know you don't want my advice, but perhaps a strong wind is really all you need," he said.

"Is there a reason you talk in riddles? I never get any real answers from you. Theron, I am starting to question if you actually even know anything."

Theron turned to me with the most serious face he had ever shown and said, "Yes, there is a very important reason I talk in riddles. The reason is that it is fun watching people torment themselves trying to figure out what I mean," Theron said, with a cocky grin on his face, confirming that this was nothing more than a joke to him.

He was short on compassion, but knowing what he went through in the arena, it was no surprise to me. In reality, Theron had faced many horrors in his life. Before he turned to leave he said, "I think you should stay home tonight and keep yourself out of trouble."

The people in town were busy hanging decorations and getting prepared for the festival. Once back at the inn, Avery said the day before a package had come for me. Nessa had put it away, and as soon as I walked through the door, she ran to get it. There was a note that read, "This was your mother's. She would want you to have it," but it did not say who it was from. I opened the package and saw a long white pretty dress. It was made of the softest material I had ever felt, and it had delicate gold detailing. I tried it on. It was too big and did not fit right in some places. Nessa used some white thread to take in the dress so it fit me properly. Her old hands were quick with a needle and thread. I gave Avery some of the money I had earned from retrieving the journal and told her to buy a new dress for the festival.

Avery's and Nessa's spirits were already high having sold out of all their herbs, tincture, and medicines to the large crowds who were in town for the festival. The festival was being set up in a meadow because it was the biggest open area that could hold all of the town's people. That night, I freshened up and put on my mother's white dress. We all walked to the meadow where children were running around chasing fireflies. I smiled looking down at Kat in my arms, thinking one day she would be chasing fireflies with the other children. Music was playing, people were dancing, and the sound of laughter filled the air. The end-of-summer breeze carried the music to every corner of the festivities. There was a seafood buffet and white wine. After I held Kat for a while, Nessa took her from my arms.

Amos walked over to me with a mouth full of food and said, "The food is always the best at festivals." But his mouth was so full I could barely understand a word, and every time he opened his mouth, a small piece of food would come flying out.

"I have impeccable taste, and of all the other dragons, I am the best at throwing parties," a voice said from beside us.

Amos and I turned our heads and saw Liam standing there with a smug look on his face.

Amos said, "Yeah," and some other words I couldn't make out.

I had to laugh looking at him. He had a glob of white tartar sauce on his chin. I never knew anyone who was so oblivious to having food on their face. It seemed as if every time he eats, he was incapable of feeling the runaway food on his face. Liam seemed not to notice. When I looked at Avery, she was rolling her eyes.

I pointed to Amos's chin and said, "You have a visitor."

He put his hand over his mouth and said, "Sorry," before running away in search of a napkin.

I turned to Liam, who was talking to a tall man who I did not know, and asked, "Where's Kyra?"

Liam replied in a disappointed yet irritated tone, "Kyra was not feeling well, so she decided to stay home unfortunately."

I looked around and saw no other dragons or dragonesses and asked, "Where are the others?"

Liam frowned and said, "His Majesty King Maverick had some last-minute things to do, so he can't make it tonight, and Willow's people are still sick, so she is tending to them the best she can. Ann isn't allowed to come to events after she sunk Atlantis. Theron is at the bar having a drink."

I could sense a bit of disappointment behind his words. I put on a smile and said, "Why don't you tell me how you planned the best festival I've ever been to."

I was not lying. I couldn't remember any parties or festivals in my past.

He then grew a big prideful smile and said, "I know Willow couldn't even plan this event as well as I can."

I stood there smiling and nodding every so often, because no matter how boring the conversation was, it was still nice seeing Liam happy. After a while, I felt a tap on my shoulder. I turned to see Avery with two glasses of champagne in her hands. She held one of the glasses out in front of me, offering it to me.

"No, thank you. I don't drink," I stated plainly.

Liam piped up and said, "If she doesn't want it, I will take it."

"Sure," Avery said and handed it to him as he gladly took it.

I turned to him and said, "I didn't know you drank."

Liam smiled and said, "Although I prefer water, I only drink on special occasions, and when I do, it is only a glass or two, mostly for show, unlike some drunks I know." The last part was clearly referring to Theron.

"So what are you two talking about?" Avery asked.

"Well, I was telling Bora how I put together this festival all by myself," he said.

"Bora, can you do something for me?" Avery said.

I looked at Avery skeptically and said, "Sure. What is it?"

Avery hesitantly said, "Well, you see Amos has never had the best of luck with girls," while pointing in the direction of Amos.

He was over at one of the buffet tables trying to flirt with a tan dirty-blonde woman in a flowy orange dress. He was so nervous you could see a little sweat dripping down his forehead. He moved one of his hands too close to the buffet table in front of him, because I was pretty sure he had no idea what to do with it. He accidentally knocked over a bowl of cocktail sauce, splashing the woman's dress. Both their eyes widened as they looked at the cocktail sauce splashed all over her dress. He then looked her dead in the eyes and opened his mouth ready to say something, most likely an apology, but before he could, she threw her drink in his face before storming off.

"Yes, I can see that," I said, feeling bad for poor Amos.

"Can you please go dance with him?" she asked.

I looked back at Amos as he was looking for something to dry his face. I walked over to an empty table and grabbed a napkin and headed straight toward him. I handed it to him, and he thanked me instantly. Once he was done drying himself off, I extended one of my hands out in front of him. He looked down at my hand for a moment, then looked up into my eyes confused.

"Would you like to dance?" I asked him.

The moment those words left my lips, his entire face lit up, and he replied, "Yes, yes. I'd love to dance with you!" before grabbing my hand and dragging me onto the dance floor.

I put one of my hands on his shoulder and the other in his hand as we started to dance. After only a few seconds, I accidentally stepped on his foot as he winced in pain.

"Sorry," in a panic, I said, not entirely knowing what I was doing.

Amos smiled, "It's not a problem. Personally, I'm not the best dancer either."

We both laughed. After a little while, I got the hang of it. Liam and Avery stood off to the side watching us and talking. Nessa was off somewhere, most likely with Kat watching some children playing, while the only thing going through my mind at the moment was that, for the first time in who knows how long, everything felt right in the world, nothing to worry about, nothing to fear, and most importantly, nothing to question.

Unfortunately, this feeling all too quickly vanished just as quickly as it had come. Suddenly a dark purple mist rolled in. At first, I thought it was some kind of fog. I didn't think much of it until it surrounded us. It felt as if I was up to my neck in quicksand, and soon everyone there could not move below their necks.

Then an all-too-familiar voice spoke, "Well, well, well, just the girl I wanted to see."

I turned my head and saw the hag walking toward me. Her arm that was cut off had been sewn back on, but it was backward. She walked closer to me with a sickly sweet grin on her face. I looked around in a panic, not sure what she was going to do. Everyone around me was immobile, unable to move. I looked around, hoping to see one of the dragons. I was even desperate enough to accept help from Theron, but he was nowhere in sight. She put her backward arm on my face, holding my face still. Next thing I knew, I felt an immense pain in my right eye as she ripped it out of its now throbbing socket with her good arm. Her smile grew as she looked at my eye in her hand. She then took a black stone out of her pocket.

"With your eye and a stone from the River Styx, I can finally complete my end of the deal." And she began to chant. "Aingeal, aingeal, aingeal, aingeal, aingeal. . ."

My eye and the stone started to levitate until a bright light flashed. The black stone now had a hole in the middle, and the black stone changed its color to a light gray as it combined with my eye. My eye now sat in the hole in the middle of the stone. The next thing I knew, the levitating stone/eye had fallen and landed in her hand.

I started thinking of ways to free myself and the others when she said, "Now, I'll rip out the other one for good measure."

I tried to think calmly and took a deep breath. Then the wind started to blow hard, making the purple smoke disappear. I was dropped on my feet, no longer being held up by the purple fog.

I started walking toward her, and I said, "If this is the game you want to play, fine; I'll play."

My scales reappeared and started spreading along my arm and neck. She suddenly looked paler than the moon itself, if it were somehow possible. She clenched the stone in her hand and ran in fear. I chased after her making sure she was in my sight at all times. The hag ran into the Ruinous Forest. There were signs all around it saying "Danger, Do Not Enter" and "Turn Back Now." I didn't care. I just wanted to get my eye back and get some answers, and I didn't care what it took to get them. I felt as if my mind was drowning in an ocean of questions and not a dry land of answers in sight. I could no longer see the hag, and I was about to run after her when Liam in his dragon form appeared in front of me. He shifted back in his human form, his hand stretched out in front of him, pushing me back and then holding me in a tight hug. I felt nothing but anger, and all I wanted was to get my hands on that old hag.

I looked up at him and yelled, "Why did you stop me?"

Liam stared at me and said, "The forest is a maze that no one but dragons can escape, and we still don't know what you are. If you had run after her, you would have eventually lost her and most importantly yourself in there."

I was about to argue when I heard the sound of heavy feet nearby. I turned my head and saw an out-of-breath Amos coming straight toward me. He stopped right in front of me, almost running me over.

He was panting and almost out of breath and asked, "Are you ok?"

I looked at him and said, "No, I am not ok! Some old hag just ripped out my eye—"

And before I could finish, he put his lips on mine. I was taken aback. I did not expect this reaction from Amos. After a few seconds, I pulled away and slapped him across the face.

Amos yelled, "What did you do that for?"

"When someone is freaking out, the first thing you do is kiss them?" I yelled.

"I thought it would help," he said.

More frustrated, I yelled, "How the hell would getting kissed by you help with anything? That hag took my eye." Amos said, "I don't know. It was an impulse."

I glared at him and said in a low voice, "If you ever attempt that again, you're as good as dead. You understand me?"

Amos gulped and said, "Yes, I understand you, Bora."

I heard rustling noises behind me. I turned and saw Avery running toward me, tackling me into a tight hug.

She held me tightly and said, "Don't ever run off like that again."

At that point, I felt like a small child who had wandered away from their mother. She grabbed my face and inspected where my eye used to be.

"Does it hurt?"

"Yes! Of course, it hurts. Right now it is throbbing, but I am sure it looks pretty bad. I am now a one-eyed monster. Is it bleeding?" I asked.

"It seems to have stopped, but it is hard to tell. The whole right side of your face is covered with blood."

"I will have Nessa look at it as soon as we get back home," I said.

She glanced at Amos and saw blood smeared on the left side of his face and blood coming from the right side of his lip from where I had slapped him. She looked confused and asked, "What happened to Amos?"

Amos and I both stayed quiet, not really sure what to say. We had completely forgotten Liam was there.

And with an amused look on his face, "I can answer that; your brother kissed Bora," Liam said.

At that, Avery's eyes widened and her mouth fell open. Liam then explained that Bora had freaked out and slapped him in the face. Everyone was quiet again. The only noises around were the sounds of crickets and an owl hooting. Then the sound of tearing could be heard as Avery ripped a piece of her new red dress off and tied it over my head, making an improvised eye patch.

"Why did you do that to your new dress? You didn't have to do that," I said.

Avery smiled and said, "It's just a dress, and I am not used to your new look yet. You, Amos, and the others are the most important people in my life right now, and I can't stand to see you hurt."

We all went back to get Nessa and Kat and headed off for home.

As he walked back, Liam said, "Bora, I am sorry I wasn't able to help you back there in the tent, but I was also affected by the fog and I could not move. Don't worry; we'll find the old hag and make her pay. This has been a crazy night. That fog spell was very powerful; no one would be able to break free of it. Maybe if Maverick were here, he could have done so. Kyra will be upset that she missed it," Liam said.

When we got back to the festival, it was completely empty, except for Nessa, Kat, and Theron. Nessa was sitting in a chair and looked panicked. As we got closer, I could see her let out her breath in relief. Theron, at the bar, was passed out, to no one's surprise. Liam walked over to Theron and shook him slightly. Theron groggily spat out some nonsense that no one could understand.

Liam backed up with a disgusted look on his face and said, "You see this, Bora? Let this be a lesson: Alcohol will only make you happy temporarily. It does nothing but inflict permanent consequences on your life. Well, this has been a little more than interesting. Bora, I am sorry for what has happened to you. We will find that hag." Liam turned and left.

I looked at Theron and walked over to the bar. I got him a glass of water and what I believed was a piece of sourdough bread and placed it on the counter in front of him. Then we all left.

At home, I washed the blood from my face and Nessa cleaned my now-empty eye socket. She used some oil of oregano to fight off infection and made me some turmeric, ginger, and devil's claw tea to reduce inflammation and pain.

I lay in bed that night and wondered, *Why?* Why did that old hag hate me so much, and what did she know about me and my past? Finally, I drifted off to sleep.

CHAPTER 8

The Aftermath

AFTER THE INCIDENT AT THE festival, Nessa sewed a proper eye patch for me. The next day, I showed up to work; it was storming and there weren't that many ships in the harbor.

I was in the middle of helping unload a ship when my boss, Henry, who was the second in command, came up to me and said, "The big boss wants to see you."

I had never met the big boss. Henry had always been the person I answered to, and he had always been more than fair to me. I turned to him and thanked him before heading to the big boss's office. I exited the boat dock and crossed the street and walked to a brick building that was painted white but was now a dingy gray. I tried to open the heavy metal door, but the wind refused to let me inside. After a short fight, I was able to enter the building. I walked into the lobby area where customers paid to dock their boats and have them unloaded. At the front desk sat a old tired woman named Helen who obviously did not get paid enough by her small frame and old clothing.

I walked over to her and said, "Hey, Helen. The—"

But before I could finish, she raised her wrinkly, bony hand with extremely long fingernails and said, "Go up the staircase. It's the third door on the left. Mr. Muc is waiting for you," without looking up from the book she was reading.

I said, "Thank you," before heading up the spiral metal staircase.

When I got to the top, I walked down a narrow hallway. I followed Helen's directions and went to the third door on the left. I stood in front of the door for a moment, trying to brace myself for whatever I was about to face. I tightened my hand into a fist and knocked on the door.

A gruff voice said, "Come in."

When I entered, I made sure to close the door behind me. In front of me sat a man so plump I was surprised he could make it through the hallway to get up here. The desk looked miniature, as half of his large body was displayed from behind the desk. He had his dark brown hair parted weirdly, a little too far over to the right side of his head to hide the fact he was balding at an early age. His big nose and ears would have made a donkey jealous. He had a thick mustache that took up his entire upper lip. The buttons on his buttoned-up white shirt and vest looked like they would come flying off at any moment. His mid-length black pants were stained from food and looked like they were strangling his chubby legs. In his big mouth was a cigar that he was trying to light with what looked like a gold lighter. I took a seat in the dark leather chair in front of him.

"So, Mr. Muc, you wanted to see me."

Mr. Muc raised one of his chubby hands, letting me see his sausage fingers were covered in gold and diamond rings. "Mr. Muc is my father's name. Call me Sir Muc."

I rephrased my question by saying, "My apologies, Sir Muc—"

But before I could finish speaking, Sir Muc started hacking, allowing me to see his disgusting lemon-yellow stained teeth. After about six hacks, he spit something into a bucket nearby, and it landed with a loud clunk. I looked away from him, trying to hide my urge to vomit.

Then Sir Muc said, "Listen, Bora, you must be wondering why I called you here."

"Yes, that's right," I said, trying to keep a straight face.

"Well, Bora, you are famous around here. All the men who work on the ships with you say that you are the strongest woman they have ever met and the most hard working, but unfortunately you are no longer needed here!"

"Sir Muc, I don't understand. Why are you letting me go?"

Sir Muc then raised one of his sausage fingers to shush me and said, "Ok, I'll be blunt with you. After the little incident at the Phoenix Festival, you seem to be a liability and a hazard to my business. People no longer feel safe working with you, and no one wants you around. So from today on, you are no longer welcome here, girly. Goodbye."

I looked at him for a moment before realizing something. I said, "You were going to fire me a while ago, but you kept me here longer just to use me while it was busy. Now that winter is coming, you're getting rid of me the first chance you get."

In an irritated voice, Sir Muc said, "You're lucky I even considered giving you this job in the first place. A woman's job is being married and tending to her children, not loading and unloading cargo ships!" I chuckled as Sir Muc asked, "What is so funny?"

"It's understandable why a man with such wealth is still single—because you are nothing more than a narcissistic, sexist, repulsive pig of a man who will never get a wife even if you paid someone to marry you," I said.

Sir Muc's face was now bright red, making him look more like a pig. He pointed one of his sausage fingers at me again and said, "Get out."

I stood up and walked out of the door, but before closing the door, I turned to him and said, "Oink oink."

Right after that, I slammed the door shut as fast as possible. Sir Muc must have grabbed one of the books from the corner of his desk, and he threw it at the door as it hit the door with a loud thud before falling to the floor. Helen looked at me befuddled as I made my way down the stairs.

I looked her dead in the eyes and said, "Just quit already. He will never pay you enough to retire," before kicking the door open, causing it to hit the wall behind it. Helen looked surprised. I stopped once I was in the doorway and said, "Can I give you a message for Mr. Muc?" Helen hesitated before nodding. "Please tell Sir Pig upstairs that he is a dimwit for me, would you?"

I didn't even wait for her response; I slammed the door and started walking away. I walked across the street before turning back and taking one final look at the building. I looked up toward the window and saw Sir Muc glaring at me. I put the biggest smile on my face and walked away and headed for home.

On the way home, the sky opened up and it started to rain hard, but it felt good as it cooled my anger.

When I got home, Nessa said, "You look like a drowned cat."

I told Nessa that I had lost my job.

She said, "Don't worry; there are plenty of jobs out there for someone like you," and she made me a chamomile and lavender tea.

Amos and I were still not on good terms after the Phoenix Festival. I couldn't help but feel bad every time I looked at him; he reminded me of a beaten puppy. It was his fault for kissing me. I had only reacted that way because he had caught me off guard. I had never thought of him that way, and I am not sure how I feel about him now.

About a week after I was fired, Nessa gave me the task of accompanying Amos and helping him collect and sell firewood while I continued to look for a job with a more stable income. At the break of dawn, I followed Amos into the woods, and we spent all morning chopping firewood. Amos and I barely spoke at all. I was grateful that the woods were filled with the sweet songs of the birds. Their music floated in the air and landed softly in my ears. We had lost track of time, and by late afternoon, we had two very hefty stacks of firewood. These woods were the complete opposite of the Ruinous Forest at the Phoenix Festival. Instead of darkness, there was bright sunlight shining through the trees, and the woods were filled with wildlife of every kind that called this place home. When the late afternoon sun became visible, we collected all the wood together and tied a rope around it, holding them all in place. We walked out of the woods carrying our heavy loads to the busy streets of the village. Amos walked ahead of me by a few steps owing to his long muscular legs.

All of a sudden, I felt someone yank me into an alley by the back of my hair. When they let go of my hair, I turned around and saw a man almost twice my size standing in front of me. The only thought going through my head was I wish I had my staff with me as he started to threaten me with bodily harm if I didn't hand over all my coins. I wasn't really paying attention to what he was saying. I was trying to figure out what would be the easiest way to bring him down so I could get back to helping Amos sell the firewood. I balled my fists as I prepared to win this fight in one hit, but a voice caught me off guard.

The voice said, "You should know better than to attack a lady, you thief."

I turned my head and saw Amos standing there, back pressed against the wall of the dark alleyway.

"Oh, and what are you going to do, little man?" the thief said.

"Who are you calling a little man?" Amos asked angrily.

"Yeah, little man, what are you going to do, kiss him?" I asked.

"What the heck, Bora? You're supposed to be on my side, not mock me in front of him."

"Oh, I don't want to hear it from you, Mr. You-Don't-Know-What-Consent-Is," I said.

Amos asked, "Are you really still mad about the stupid kiss? How many times must I tell you I'm sorry?"

"I can be mad as long as I want. You can't just kiss people out of nowhere and expect everything to go back to normal. Now everything is so weird between us."

The thief just kind of stared as we bickered back and forth between ourselves. The guy then said, "Hold on—you kissed her without permission?"

Amos snapped and said, "You are literally trying to rob her. I don't want to hear another word from you."

The guy said, "You're right. My apologies, ma'am. Can you please hand over all your valuables to me?"

"No!" Amos and I yelled in unison.

"Ok, done," the guy said, pulling out a knife. "How about handing over your money and your valuables?"

Amos and I looked at him as if he was crazy, and I said, "Are you a moron?"

The knife looked very small next to the very large man, but it shined in the late afternoon sun and seemed to be extremely sharp.

"You know what, Amos?" I said. "Just get out of here. I'll handle this."

"I don't think so, Bora," Amos said bluntly.

"Fine. Be my guest," I replied.

Amos put his pile of firewood off to the side by me and then held his axe tightly in his hand as he walked toward the giant man in front of us. There was something in Amos' eyes I had never seen before. He suddenly had the eyes of a killer. The giant man froze in fear not knowing what to do. He was not used to people willing to fight; they usually just handed over the goods. He thought it would be a good idea to run away. The back of the alleyway was blocked with a huge worn-out wooden fence that had rusted barbed wire on the top of it. The man swallowed a lump in his throat, knowing his only way to escape would be to run past Amos. He ran head first toward Amos. At this point, I started to worry quite a bit. The giant man was at least a hundred pounds heavier than Amos. Amos was going to be trampled if I did not step in soon, and my worries intensified as I saw the man get closer to him.

I was about ready to intervene when Amos ran toward the man. Amos aimed the back of his axe, forgoing the blade, at one of the guy's legs, more precisely his knee, before bringing it down hard. The man stopped running and let out a roar of pain. This gave Amos the opportunity to grab him by his throat and slam him against the wall. Amos did not lose his grip on the man's throat; in fact, it only seemed to tighten. By now tears were swelling in the corner of the giant man's eyes as he gripped on to Amos' arm that was holding his throat. Amos seemed like a different person to me at that moment. It seemed as if a coin had been flipped and this was what was hiding under his kind and silly demeanor. Then Amos looked at me from the corner of his eyes, as if suddenly remembering I was there. His eyes widened, and his hold on the man's throat loosened.

"Bora, I. . . Damn it!" Amos yelled when he let go of his hold on the man's throat.

The giant man remembered he still had his sad excuse for a knife in his hand. He used the knife to stab Amos in his hand as he had raised it to protect his body. Then the giant man ran away. Amos grabbed his arm and held his hand up. I immediately ran over to him and looked at the wound. The wound was bad, considering it went all the way through the palm of his hand. I grabbed my bag, reached in, and pulled out a bandage and some tincture and applied some yarrow oil to the cut to help clean his wound, so it would not get infected, before wrapping his hand with a bandage. By this time the sun was starting to set.

Amos said, "We should probably start heading back to the inn."

I looked over and saw our stacks of firewood were still there, not having sold any. "Avery is going to kill us," I said bluntly while looking at the firewood.

Amos' eyes followed mine as he looked at the pile. "Now, Bora, I wouldn't say that," he said.

"What do you mean? We literally did not make any coins today," I said.

Amos chuckled as he pulled out a medium-sized leather sack from his pocket. The sack had to have at least thirty coins in it.

My eyes widened at the sight of the sack, and I said, "Where did you get that?"

Amos smiled his usual wide smile and said, "Well, you see the man that was here earlier is letting us permanently borrow these."

My jaw almost dropped to the ground as I looked at Amos who seemed unfazed by the events that had just happened.

He walked past me and picked up his pile of wood with his good hand and said, "Come on."

I did not say anything as we walked back on the now almost empty streets as it was dusk. Amos was walking right next to me before stopping abruptly in front of a small shop window. I was a few feet away when I noticed he was no longer with me, before turning my head to see where he was.

I walked back over to him as I asked, "Is something wrong?"

Amos said, "Nothing really. Just looking."

I walked over to where Amos was standing and noticed he was staring at some throwing stars. They reminded me of a sharp metal snowflake. My eyes wandered over to the throwing stars' price tag and saw that they were seventeen coins.

Amos saw me eyeballing the price and said, "I know they are way overpriced. Not even coming with their own poison would justify the cost of them."

When he said that, my eyes shifted from the throwing stars and were now on him.

I asked, "What do you mean by coming with their own poison, Amos?"

Amos smiled and said, "Well, you see, throwing stars are designed to scratch you. So people rub poisons on the ends of the spikes to make them more useful."

As he talked, I smiled and listened. I thought back to when I had asked Avery about her past and she had seemed really hesitant to talk about it and joked saying, when I tell her about my past, she will tell me about her and Amos' past.

When he was done talking, I said, "Amos, can I ask you something?"

Amos immediately said, "Sure. I don't see a problem in it."

"What did you and Avery do before we met each other?"

After I asked, I saw the smile on Amos' mouth waver as if he was bothered by me asking what he and his sister did but didn't want me to know that it bothered him.

About thirty seconds later, he let out a nervous laugh and said, "It's not really important what we did before we met each other. All that matters is that we met and we all have changed for the better by meeting each other. Now let's get home before it gets any later so Avery and Nessa won't be worried."

As we walked, I kept taking quick glances at him. In my mind I continued to question their past, but decided, sooner or later, whether my memories came back or not, I would stand by their side no matter what. After all, that was the least I could do for them.

When we got back to the inn, we found everyone sitting outside in the evening's cool air. We both got an earful from Avery for staying out later than she had expected. After Amos tossed her the bag of coins, she quit complaining. As for the incident with Amos' hand, he insisted that he had accidentally cut it when we were out cutting wood.

When Nessa, Kat, and Avery headed inside, I pulled Amos back and asked, "Why did you lie to them?"

Amos looked through the open door over to his sister who was playing with Kat in her arms and said, "This world is a messed-up place. This is the first time in who knows how long I've seen Avery so happy and worry free. I wouldn't want to ruin it. Would you?"

I shook my head, and we both headed inside as I tried to forget about this conversation.

I had a hard time finding employment as a one-eyed girl. It didn't help that everyone in town had witnessed my attack from the hag and everyone was frightened by it. I eventually found a job at an overpriced secondhand goods and book shop. The owner was a tall, thin paranoid man. The funny thing was that he did not know anything about how I lost my eye. He seemed to think it was some kind of accident. He was so thin that all of his clothes looked like they could easily fall off him. He had dark skin and huge bags under his sunken eyes. He told me to call him Mr. Prids. He didn't pay much, but he was a kind man. He often left town for long periods of time in search of exotic goods and books. His shop was called Artifacts and Papyrus. My job was to inspect what he brought back from his travels and then sell the items for three times their actual value.

Now the summers in Bateau were extremely hot, but I would not be lying if I said that the winters were just as brutal. The City of Bateau became a former shell of itself owing to the loss of shipping in the frozen waters. The owner of the inn where we stayed left as soon as the snow started to fall. Everyone else in the inn left as well. So, Nessa, Kat, Avery, Amos, and I had the whole place to ourselves.

At night, we all huddled together in the lobby near the fireplace as close as we could get and worried that we would get frostbite while we slept, although it was strange that I never felt the cold. They all seemed to notice, but no one ever mentioned it to me. During the day, the cold was not much better. I continued working at Artifacts and Papyrus collecting my pay every week even though business was very slow. Mr. Prids didn't seem to care that he wasn't making any money and never complained about paying me. Nessa worked as a healer, going to people's homes and providing medicine and tinctures for their ailments. I worried about her being out in the cold weather. Some days, Avery made her stay home and Avery took over for her. Avery was becoming quite the healer herself. Every day, Amos entered the woods and cut and collected firewood. He was doing a good job keeping us well fed and warm. Avery and Amos did everything that we asked of them. They were also keeping the whole town supplied with firewood and were also taking such good care of Kat.

One morning, Nessa and I were ready to go. She wore my heavy cloak and a leather bird beak mask so that she wouldn't get sick and bring home any illness. I wore an old brown shawl that was too long for me; I believed it was once owned by a giant. Now that I think about it, it may have been old brown curtains that Nessa had found discarded. Nessa needed the warm cloak more than I did. As we walked out of the inn, it was a battle just to close the door behind us. I walked Nessa to her first home visit and continued on my way. The raging wind blew even though it was a clear bright day outside. The sun reflected off the deep white snow. With every breath I took, I was able to see the water vapor when I exhaled. All around me, people were wearing thick coats on top of layer after layer of clothing. I stood in a gray dress, black flats, and a thin brown shawl, yet I didn't feel the slightest bit cold. Every step I took on my way to work I felt the eyes of the people I passed on me. Their harsh whispers and gossip about me as I walked past them was something I had to learn to ignore ever since the Phoenix Festival. I will admit I am happy to have the job at Artifacts and Papyrus because there are hundreds of old books there for reading, and reading about the past helps me imagine my own. I don't always feel like I fit in at home. Now don't get me wrong—I love everyone in our little makeshift family, but I'm not like them. I am out in the freezing cold weather and I am fine, while the others are doing everything they can to stay warm. I passed some children running around and playing in the snow. Their red noses and chattering teeth are a reminder that I am different.

At Artifacts and Papyrus, I again struggled to close the door behind me from the raging wind. It was warm inside with an old musty smell you could almost taste. I dusted off the snow that was clinging to me, and I cleaned up the snow that I had dragged in. I picked up a pile of books and brought them over and lit a small fire. I sat on a stool and started reading through them. The first book was called *The History of Magic Artifacts, and Tools*. There was a chapter on dragon artifacts that explained that dragon scales were practically indestructible. Dragon scales will always grow back, and if their scales fall out, and will grow back twice as strong. I wondered if this was true. I knew that Theron was missing some of his scales, and I wondered why they had not grown back. As I continued to read, I found more interesting facts. For example, Moon Lilies, a type of plant with the scientific name Ipomoea alba, was poisonous to humans and animals and can cause death except for dragons; dragons can become severely weakened and can get very sick, but it was unlikely that they will die. All parts of Moon Lilies were poisonous, including their roots, stems, leaves, nectar, seeds, and even its pollen. As I continued to read through the book, I noticed there were several chapters missing.

A chapter called the "Adder Stone" got my interest. As I started to read, I saw what had happened to me play back in my mind. It said that the adder stone was made from the eye of someone who was special. It was made from a stone from the River Styx and an eye of someone with the gift. The next few pages were missing, but what kind of gift? The next page went on to say that the Styx stone works like a holder with a hole in the middle that the gifted eye was placed in and that eye acts like a lens, making it possible for the unseen to be seen. An experienced witch or wizard used a magic spell to make the adder Stone, which was used to see the dead or to read something that was written in ancient text. In anger, I stood up and threw the book across the room. I fell to my knees and cried.

Once again, I had not received any answers; I only had more questions. The thought of someone special or someone with a gift kept going through my head. I was not either of those things. I just wanted to fit in and live a normal life like that of my friends. *I am tired of trying to figure out who I am or what I am. What did I do to be tormented in such a way?* I tried to stop my tears, but the harder I tried, the more tears came rolling down my face. I was so upset that my body was shaking, and it wouldn't stop. I grabbed my shawl and wrapped it around me tightly for comfort. I lay down by the fire, and before I knew it, I nodded off to sleep.

CHAPTER 9

A Family of My Own

I WOKE UP FROM MY sleep, and four hours had passed. I realized how late it was and I needed to get home so no one would worry about me. I quickly picked up the pile of scattered books and headed for home. The wind howled, and the snowflakes whipped my face. I walked home slowly, enjoying the blizzard-like snowy day. I stood still and closed my one eye, taking in the quiet still of the day. When I opened my eye, everything seemed whiter, like I was walking through a cloud, but everything looked identical. I could barely tell up from down. I sighed and hoped Nessa was already home.

I saw a black object moving in the snow. It was the cat that had led me to Nessa! It seemed to have just woken up from a nap, like what I was doing not too long ago. The cat stretched, then walked away, and I followed it. The storm blew harder and harder, and it was getting more difficult to see what was right in front of me. The cat slowed down, acting as a guide through the blinding snow, which got me thinking, *Did the cat lose me on purpose when I first met him?* I felt anger rising in me. *Enough with the questions, or else I might go mad before I get a single answer.* As I continued to follow the cat, we came across an old brick building, the inn. It was now starting to get dark, and it would get colder. The cat was standing next to me, its eyes not leaving as it stared contently at the door.

I turned to the cat and said, "Thank you. Do you want to come in?"

The cat meowed and turned its back toward me and walked away. I did the same. I walked over to the door, let out a deep breath, and when I turned around, I did not see the cat or any footprints other than my own. I shrugged and thought that they might have already filled up with the snow. I pulled the door as hard as I could, but it would not budge. I pulled harder, but it still wouldn't budge. I pulled it even harder; the wind was making it almost impossible for the door to open. The last pull caused the door to hit the wall with a loud bang, causing everyone inside the room to jump. Kat started crying, while Avery and Amos were staring at me, not saying a word. Nessa was in the only comfortable chair by the fire, fast asleep. Hitting the door so hard allowed a bunch of snow to get inside. I pushed as much snow as I could out, and then I closed the door behind me. I walked over and picked up Kat, holding her close to me and soothing her.

In an annoyed voice, Avery said, "You're almost an hour and a half hour late."

I mumbled and said, "Sorry," not wanting to get in a fight.

"Pardon, I couldn't hear you," Avery said.

Right now I was screaming in my head and on the verge of seeing red. "It has been a long day," I said. I took a deep breath and bit my tongue, not wanting anger to cloud my judgment and cause me to say something I would regret. I turned my head to her and said, "Sorry," loud enough for everyone to hear but quiet enough not to disturb Nessa.

Avery sighed and said, "Why were you so late anyway?"

I was about to reply when I was cut off by a loud slurp. We both slowly turned our heads to see Amos eating beef stew and enjoying watching us argue. We glared at him, our eyes shifting to each other and then to him. Then there was silence when Amos got the hint that he wasn't welcome. He put his spoon down, picked up the bowl in both hands, and started drinking it. The stew was so hot it burned his mouth. He ripped the bowl away from his mouth, then spotted a small pile of snow by the door and grabbed a handful of it and shoved it in his mouth. He then grabbed another small handful of snow and put it in his stew and chugged the rest of the stew down. There was another moment of silence as we tried to comprehend what we had just witnessed.

Avery yelled and said, "Why didn't you tell us that the stew was done? I haven't eaten all day."

Amos went to get us bowls and spoons. Our loud voices made Kat cry again. As soon as Kat started crying, Avery rushed over to

Kat and held out her arms, and Kat reached for her. Avery cooed at her and rubbed her back comforting her.

I said, "I'm going to freshen up," before leaving the room.

I walked down the hallway as Amos walked past me, arms full of wooden bowls and spoons.

He stopped and said, "How are you?"

"I am ok," I said. "Just a rough day."

"You look tired," he said. "Don't be long. The stew is good and hot."

I continued to the bathroom and locked the door behind me. I looked in the mirror at my reflection. Up one side of my neck, there were faded gray scales. I turned on the tap and splashed some water on my face. I took some deep breaths, trying to calm my nerves. I said to myself, "What are you?" Then I turned off the water and looked back up in the mirror. When I opened my eye again and looked in the mirror, all the scales were gone. I let out one final sigh of relief, but something felt somehow off. I heard a noise at the door. I looked over and saw the doorknob turning as if someone was trying to open it.

"It's occupied," I said, but the doorknob seemed to turn faster now.

Soft knocking followed, as if the person on the other side of the door refused to leave. I stood quietly not making a sound, and the door handle started to move again.

"Who is there?" I asked.

I braced my hands on the door in case they tried to force it open. After a few minutes, I heard what sounded like someone sneaking away from the bathroom door. I waited a few more minutes and opened the door slowly and cautiously stepped out into the hallway before closing the door behind me. I walked back to the main room where everyone was sitting.

I said, "The bathroom is empty now. Whoever was trying to get in, you can use it."

Everyone stared at me.

Amos said, "None of us has left the room. If someone tried to get in, it wasn't one of us."

Avery was eating her stew, so I sat down next to her, and Amos handed me a bowl of stew. I sat there staring at it for a few minutes.

Amos said, "I am going to take a look around and make sure all the doors are locked," and off he went.

Avery whispered in my ear, "Don't worry; I made the stew."

I took my first bite, and the stew somehow made me feel normal again. It was good and just what I needed. The color was an appetizing brownish red. There were pieces of beef, potato, carrot, and celery. I took a mouthful of the thick broth that was light and hot, and the beef was practically melting in my mouth. The vegetables were soft but not too mushy. In other words, it was perfect in every way. I ate it so fast I couldn't believe that I emptied the bowl in minutes.

Avery giggled and said, "Well, it looks like someone loves my cooking."

After a few minutes, Amos came back and reported that he didn't see anyone, and he had checked and made sure that all the doors were locked.

Avery looked at me and said, "How would you like it if you and I went on a trip to get more stuff for that shop of yours?"

I looked at her confused and said, "Where might that be?"

Avery smiled and said, "I think we should go back in time and visit everywhere you have been and see what we find."

I didn't know what to say, so I just sat there and thought for a moment.

Avery's smile widened, and she said, "Come on; think about it. You might just find some answers to all of your questions."

"Don't listen to her, Bora. My sister is always meddling in business that she doesn't belong in," Amos said.

Avery gave him a glare like she wanted to hit him.

I sighed and said, "Alright, Avery. Let's go to the abandoned library. I want to see if I can find a book on the adder stone."

Avery smiled victoriously over winning the argument with her brother. Amos pouted. Nessa said, "It's getting late. Time for bed."

None of us argued with her. They all huddled by the fire to keep warm, I stayed away since I tend to not feel the cold. I was the last one to fall asleep; it probably didn't help that I had fallen asleep at work. I just lay there staring at the ceiling, thinking about everything that was happening. I was worried about what I might find out about myself. I looked around the room, smiled, and thought, *These people are my family. They'll stick with me no matter what I find out.* Then finally I drifted off to sleep.

CHAPTER 10

Back to the Library

AVERY AND I DIDN'T LEAVE until March because I was sick for a week with a minor cold that caused Amos to somehow get pneumonia and you can't leave an infant with a sick person. Speaking of Kat, she was starting to crawl and babble more. Her dark hair was starting to grow in. I enjoyed watching her grow. She was like a sapling, and I was watching her become a tree before my very eye. I'd be lying if I said being around her didn't fill my heart with joy, because it does, she was so adorable and I can't help but smile and feel happy when I am around her.

I asked my boss Mr. Prids at Artifacts and Papyrus if I could go on the trip to search for books from Vor Langer.

His face lit up with joy, and he said, "Bora, you have just made me so happy, and I am looking forward to seeing what you bring back for me."

He had recently hurt his leg and couldn't go on adventures and collect new exotic goods and books for the shop. Most of the snow had melted, but it was still cold outside. People were starting to come back to Bateau but not as many as were once here. We left in the morning to make the most out of the daylight. I brought the brown shawl and my scythe, and Avery had her cloak and bow. This journey felt as if I was going full circle, having gone to Arm where I had picked up the journal and now heading back to Vor Langer. All I needed to do was find the hag that tried to kill me and took my eye from me.

Once we reached the forest, it started to rain. We tried to find the mom manticore's den to take shelter until the rain stopped, but we were unable to find it. Avery kept getting us lost, and that was when I learned she had no sense of direction. When we finally did find the den, we were soaking wet after hours of being rained on. When we went into the den, the momma was grooming one of her cubs while the other two playfully fought each other. They were so much bigger than the last time we had seen them. The mom stopped and looked up at us, then went back to what she was doing. Her cubs tackled me and Avery to the ground. That night we mostly played with the cubs while the momma slept.

The next morning, when we woke up, we noticed that the momma and the cubs were gone. We left the den to continue our journey to Vor Langer. The forest smelled earthy from the rain; it was almost overwhelming. We found the momma manticore down the trail, sitting by a cliff with her cubs, when all of a sudden the cubs jumped off the side of the cliff and their mother just sat there and watched. I ran over to the cliff's edge expecting to see three dead manticore cubs, but looking over the edge, all I saw were three cubs flying.

Avery walked over to me and put her hand on my shoulder and said, "It looks like everyone is growing up."

All I could do was smile and nod, watching them fly for what could have been their very first time.

We continued our journey. Once we reached Vor Langer, Avery and I started looking for any information that could help me answer some of my questions. We stayed there for two days looking through books and scrolls, but we did not find one piece of information to help me. Several hundred books and scrolls had been damaged or destroyed by the rain and snow that had entered from the hole in the roof created by the hag. On the second day, I saw an old book in a corner. It was covered with so much dust that the dull yellow book looked almost white. I picked it up, wiped the dust off it, and sneezed. The title was *The History of the Royal Family*, in gold ink. I opened the book and saw a picture of the redheaded girl from the portrait at the castle. The first chapter was about Queen Phoenix who had united all the lands and become the first queen of Inue at the age of twenty. She had led her people into war against the Minotaurs. She was assassinated at the age of twenty-three after an engagement to the Minotaur general that turned out to be a trap. As I turned to the next chapter, I was shocked by what I saw. There was a woman with black hair, blue eyes, and the Kiseru that the hag had had in her hand. The Kiseru was the long, thin silver pipe the hag had used to create the purple smoke that did not allow anyone to move. The background of the picture had the same purple smoke, the same kind that had squeezed me like a python. Flashbacks to that night flooded my mind. I turned the pages of the chapter until I reached the part about the Kiseru. I read the final lines: After Queen Zenas' passing, the Kiseru was locked in the treasure room of the castle in memory of the second queen's death. Only the royal family could open that room. I did not speak, only reread that line over and over again. *The Kiseru is supposed to be in the castle, and only a royal family member can get to it.*

I thought that something didn't seem right about King Maverick when I last met with him. He must be working with the witch that ripped out my eye! Angry tears started to roll down my face, thinking that someone I trusted would hurt me in such a way. At that moment, I felt nothing but anger and frustration.

"Bora, are you alright?" Avery said behind me.

I did not turn around, not wanting her to see me in my weakened state.

"Bora?" she said again and put her hand on my shoulder.

I slowly turned my head toward her while the last couple of tears rolled down my cheek. She spoke in a soft voice as a light breeze blew and said, "Bora, what's wrong?"

I lied and said, "Nothing," wiping the last couple of tears off my face.

She looked at me, clearly concerned.

I walked past her and said, "Let's finish looking through the books and go."

We had found several interesting books and scrolls that would be good for the store. When we finished, I knotted up a scarf into a basket so it would be easier to carry our finds. With everything in hand, we were on our way back home to Bateau.

On our way back, we were quiet. We barely said a word to each other.

That night, after eating some fish that Avery caught for us, she sat down next to me and said, "Do you mind telling me why you have been so quiet?"

I hesitated and then told her, "I think King Maverick was working with the hag that ripped out my eye."

In a moment, her soft voice turned into anger, and she yelled, "That bastard! Why do you think that?"

I replied by saying, "I don't know. In one of the books I found it said the Kiseru, the one the hag used to render us unable to move, was in the picture with Queen Zena and it is kept in the treasure room at the castle and only a member of the royal family can retrieve it."

Avery tried to calm down a bit and growled then said, "Bora, those books are over three hundred years old. We are not even sure if that is true nowadays."

I just looked at her and said, "The book said the Kiseru was placed in the treasure room in memory of the second queen. It would be a treasured artifact. Why would they ever let it out of the castle?"

Avery looked at me and said, "Bora, don't believe everything you read, and don't believe everything people tell you.

You are going to find out. I wonder if Theron would know?"

The next day, we arrived back in Bateau. I told Avery to go home as I had a few errands to do real quick. I gave her the books and scrolls that were wrapped in the shawl, and we went our separate ways. I walked very fast, and every once in a while, I would turn my head to look back to see if Avery was following me. I took off running to the ocean. Once I reached the beach, I ran as fast as I could. My heart and my head were pounding so hard it was all I could hear. I stopped once I reached the familiar white marble house. I walked up the steps and knocked on the door very loudly. After a moment of nothing, I knocked even louder. Liam opened the door with his head held high and a big grin on his face.

With the sun directly behind me, he squinted his eyes and said, "Kyra, I knew you would come crawling back. Your manners have improved, though we both said some things neither of us meant, so if you apologize I'll forgive you and let you live here with me again."

I really didn't know what to say. He just stood there staring at me. Then his entire mood changed, and he now looked very disappointed.

"It's me, Bora," I said. "I am not Kyra."

He said in a sad voice that he wasn't even trying to hide, "You're not Kyra?"

I nodded and said, "You're right. I am Bora, Liam."

"The damn sun is in my eyes. My apologies, Bora," he said.

"I am sorry; did I come at a bad time?" I said. "Did you and Kyra get into a fight?"

He did not answer, but instead, he bitterly said, "What can I do for you?"

I looked at him and said, "I need a ride to the castle."

Liam looked at me and said, "Now tell me why would I do that?"

I replied, "Think how mad Kyra would be finding out you went on a trip and you don't miss her at all, instead of you just sitting here and sulking until she returns."

"Fine." He grabbed a pen and wrote, "I am out on a trip with Bora." He smiled and said, "That will make her jealous."

We walked outside, and he shifted into his dragon form. I was about to climb on his back when I heard yelling. I turned my head and saw Avery running down the beach toward us. When Avery reached us, she was out of breath, gasping for air.

The only words I could make out were "I'm coming along, too."

I turned to her and said, "No, you are not."

She gave me a frustrated look and said, "Bora, you are not leaving me behind. I am coming with you." I was about to protest again when she said, "If your theory is correct, I wouldn't mind smacking him in the face."

Liam looked confused and said, "Who are you hitting?"

Avery was about to reply when he put one of his claws near her face and said, "Never mind. I don't want to know. Just hurry up, ladies; we don't have all day for you two to argue." Liam stopped for a moment and said, "Is this what people see when they see Kyra and me fighting?"

We didn't answer, but I said, "Fine. You can come with us."

We both climbed on Liam's back, and in minutes, he took off.

I turned and asked her, "What did you do with the books and scrolls?"

"I left them at the inn for safekeeping," she replied.

"How did you find me?" I asked.

She said that she knew exactly where I was heading. The rest of the trip was quiet, not one of us saying a word. When we landed, we saw King Maverick talking to a redheaded woman. It was Kyra. She was holding a large notepad and was writing things down on a piece of paper. Liam shifted back into his human form, and we started to walk over to where they were talking.

We overheard Kyra say, "I think we should go with red."

Liam was no longer being quiet and biting his tongue. He yelled and said, "Kyra, what are you doing here?" while glaring at her.

Kyra had a smug smile on her face and said, "Liam, I thought you knew I would be helping King Maverick with the twentieth jubilee celebration."

Liam laughed and said, "That is the funniest thing you ever said. You wouldn't know style if it hit you on the head."

King Maverick placed his hand on Kyra's shoulder and said, "I am tired of hearing you two fighting. I have an idea—why don't you two talk it out with the girl you brought, while I have a little chat with Bora?"

King Maverick then grabbed my hand, dragging me away from the three of them. I turned back to see Avery's worried face not taking her eyes off of me. He dragged me to the rose garden where he showed me a new statue commissioned and placed in the garden. It was the representation of Queen Sada from the portrait, except now she was in life-size form.

King Maverick looked at the statue and said, "She was the most beautiful woman I have ever met. It is a shame her beauty will never walk in this world again." He then turned and picked the most perfect white rose. He carefully twisted the rose's stem and winced in pain.

When King Maverick winced, I asked, "Are you alright, Your Majesty?"

"No need to worry. I am perfectly fine," King Maverick replied.

He looked at his hand and saw one of the rose's thorns had cut his hand, drawing out a thin line of blood. King Maverick then made his way back to the statue and placed the rose by Queen Sada's feet.

King Maverick turned to me and said, "How rude of me—I have never told you her name, right?"

I hesitated before shaking my head no slowly. Kyra had told me who she was, but I didn't want to spoil the moment for him.

He smiled and said, "Sada. Her name was Sada."

"She was very beautiful. It must have been hard for you to lose someone who you loved so much," I said.

We stood there for a few minutes.

"I have a question I want to ask you."

He gave me a curious look and said, "Go ahead and ask."

I hesitated and said, "I know that the Kiseru the hag used to rip out my eye was supposed to be locked in the castle."

"The Kiseru was stolen from the treasure room about a week before the festival. That is the reason I did not attend the festival because there were sightings of the hag in Vex, and because Kyra was sick, and I wanted to go check Vex to see if I could find the hag. The day after the festival, Theron found the hag dead in the Ruinous Forest." He sighed again and said, "Her head was cut off from her body."

My eye went wide, and I said, "What happened to the adder stone?"

He stared at me and said, "How do you know what it is called?"

I replied and said, "I read about the adder stone in a book at the shop called Artifacts and Papyrus where I work.

"King Maverick, do you know what the adder stone is and what it is used for?"

He replied, "There is an old book in the royal library about it, and Theron said that the adder stone was not with the hag's body."

"Do you know where Theron is? I want to talk to him," I said.

King Maverick said, "I don't think that is a good idea, Bora."

I turned to him and said, "Why?"

"Dragons live a long, long time, and when someone dies, we have to live a long time without that person. The day Theron's love died is this week on the fifteenth, so right now he might just want to be alone."

King Maverick turned to me and said in a cheerful voice, "You should come to my twentieth jubilee celebration. After all, you only get to celebrate your first twenty years once."

I was hesitant at first but then said, "I would be honored."

In the background, we could hear yelling, which, no doubt, was Kyra and Liam still arguing with each other. King Maverick and I started to walk away when we heard a crash. We both jumped and turned around as fast as we could. Where King Maverick had been standing only seconds before, there was now a large flowerpot shattered into pieces, and the flowers lay in a pile of dirt. I looked up and saw the black cat sitting on the railing of a balcony above where the flowerpot had fallen, glaring at King Maverick.

I turned to King Maverick and said, "That cat is really mischievous."

King Maverick stared up at the balcony and said, "I hate all felines," and walked away.

I didn't know what Kyra and Liam were arguing about and I didn't care.

When I got closer, Kyra noticed me and stopped arguing and said, "I heard what happened to one of your eyes, Bora, and I am really sorry."

Liam was quiet for a moment, then said, "So you'll apologize to her but not to me?"

Kyra hissed and said, "You're right. You're always right. I'm sorry for not being at the Phoenix Festival."

"Now you're just telling me what I want to hear," Liam frowned.

"What do you want me to say?" Kyra snapped.

Liam yelled and said, "All I wanted was for you to be there for my big night and you knew this."

I was about to step in before it got to the point of no return, but it was already too late. Liam then yelled, "How can anyone be so incompetent as you and help plan the jubilee celebration!"

Kyra mumbled something while her hands were shaking in clenched fists.

Liam yelled, "Mind repeating that, Kyra?"

Kyra spoke in a calm, cold, and steady voice, "We are done. You and I are done."

The normally feisty tone in her voice was gone now, leaving behind an icy bland version of what it once was, so cold that it sent shivers down our spines. Everyone was surprised, even Liam since he had never seen this side of her before.

Then Kyra spoke again. "I'm done being your trophy and your personal improvement project. I've tried for so long to be supportive of you, but nothing I do is ever enough for you. I even dress nicer and cover up my scars because you can't handle the fact I am not defenseless, and I'm tired of playing the role of a weak damsel so you can feel more of a man. You love the idea of marrying someone high ranking for status, not me for who I am. I am someone who knows my worth, and it's far more than yours will ever be. Now leave, Liam, or I'll make you."

Liam was at a loss for words; he kept opening his mouth like a gasping fish about to say something but couldn't. That was when he noticed that Kyra was on the verge of tears.

He said, "Come on, Bora. You and the other girl, we are leaving now."

Liam shifted into his dragon form, and we were off and flying.

As we were flying, I heard King Maverick yell, "I forgot to tell you the party is on the eighteenth of April."

That night, we stopped to set up camp. The wind had started blowing strongly, and Liam said it was too dangerous for us to fly on his back.

While Avery set up camp in the woods under a large canopy of trees, I spoke to Liam and asked, "Are you stronger than Kyra?"

He was quiet for a moment before replying, "Yes. She is much more emotional than me. I left out of respect for her and respect for the man I used to be."

"What do you mean by that?" I asked.

"I was different back when we first met. Our fathers were good friends, and from a young age, we were betrothed to each other. We loved each other very much, and it appears at one point I lost sight of what really mattered to me."

"So, what are you going to do now?" I asked.

Liam leaned back and put his hands behind the back of his head and lay down on the hard ground under him. I copied what he did.

He spoke after a moment, "Now I am going to spend the rest of my life trying to be the man Kyra deserves, even if she'll never take me back. I will always love her til the day I die. Bora, let me give you some advice."

I turned my head away from the patch of sky I had been studying and asked, "Ok. What is your advice?"

"Never fight with someone you care about when you're angry, because, inevitably, you will say awful things to them just to hurt them. In other words, speaking when you're angry will make you say something you didn't mean and will always regret."

We did not talk much after that. The wind blowing through the treetops rocked us to sleep, and I slowly drifted off to a peaceful sleep.

The memories from that day were something Liam will never forget; his sleep was not as peaceful as mine. Every time he closed his eyes, the image of Kyra was there, with trembling hands and tears rolling down her face. He knew he was the cause of all her pain. Kyra did not deserve any of this. Kyra, his old friend, his fiancee—no, his love, and now he may have thrown it all away.

CHAPTER 11

The Truth Comes Out

I VOWED THAT THIS WOULD be the last trip I would go on. After this, I wouldn't go on another trip for a long, long time. I was tired of never staying in one place. I wanted to settle down and be there for Kat, to watch her grow up. Liam and Kyra had not talked to each other since their argument in the rose garden. I flew on Liam's back to King Maverick's twentieth jubilee celebration. I had a change of clothes packed for the festivities. We arrived two hours before the celebration started. When we got there, Liam and I changed into our party clothes. Liam took what felt like an eternity to get ready. He was wearing a white suit with a light blue shirt. We entered the Great Hall, and shortly after, Kyra came walking over to us. She wore a crimson red long dress. The top of it was simple with off-the-shoulder straps and had a lace up in the back. Her hair was curled and wavy. She looked perfect in it.

Liam looked gobsmacked and said, "Kyra, you look beautiful."

But Kyra ignored him like he was the most insignificant thing in the room. As for me, I wore a light-yellow dress with a matching eye patch and simple gold sandals. Nessa had made me the dress from material that Avery had found and traded for it with her herbal medicine.

Kyra turned to me and said, "Do you need help with anything, Bora?"

Liam piped in and said, "No, we have everything under control."

Kyra's icy cold voice from that day in the rose garden came back as she said, "I wasn't talking to you, Liam!"

Liam went quiet, and on the inside, he shriveled up like a leech that salt had touched.

I said, "No. Thank you for the offer. I'm good."

In less than a second, she changed back to her cheerful feisty self and said, "Ok. Let me know if you need anything or if you change your mind." Then Kyra walked away without acknowledging Liam again.

That was when I noticed Liam was glaring at me or, more specifically, at my dress.

"What's wrong?" I asked Liam.

He scrunched up his face and said, "Don't you have a better dress to wear?"

Now even more confused than ever, I said, "Pardon. What is wrong with what I am wearing?"

"Well, that style has been out of fashion for at least two decades, and since this is a very special event, I think you should wear something more fashion-forward or at least what's in style now."

I was about to say something back, but he cut me off by continuing to tell me, "You should really go brush out the animal nest on your head that you call hair. I mean, really, do you know how knotted hair gets while flying? I swear it's worse than Trista's, and I think she doesn't even know what a hairbrush is."

I stood there listening to him rant and berate me. He grabbed my arm and dragged me from the Great Hall to one of the sitting rooms where he had left his bag. From his bag, he pulled out a brush and started brushing my hair. He practically spent the next hour brushing and styling my hair before the party started.

After we entered the ballroom, Liam pulled me aside and said, "These people are high-ranking officials and members of society, so don't make a fool of yourself."

"Thanks for the vote of confidence," I said.

At that moment, I realized that Liam was right. Everyone was so nicely dressed that I started to feel a bit self-conscious. Most were a little plump, not knowing the meaning of hunger or hard work at any time in their lives. I continued to walk around a bit until I ran into a familiar face. Kyra was surrounded by a few dashing young men. I walked over to where they were all standing. It took some time to squeeze past some of the men to get to Kyra; it seemed that none of the men wanted to move or give up their spot near her. When

I reached her, she was laughing, but it wasn't her usual loud laugh. It was significantly quieter and seemed somewhat forced.

"Hello, Kyra," I said, smiling at her.

Kyra stopped laughing the very second she heard my voice and turned to me with her usual wide smile. Past Kyra's left shoulder in the distance, I could make out Liam standing in front of a pillar, his back pressed against it. Liam was glancing over at Kyra every so often. Kyra knew this because every time his eyes fell upon her, she would cling to one of the many men nearby. Every time Liam saw this, he would turn away with a hurt and defeated look in his eyes. A tiredness in his eyes held a few tears that he was holding back as well. I kind of felt bad for Liam. I thought, *I know Liam and Kyra never had, let's call it, the best of relationships, but they seemed to make each other happy. Sure Liam was boring and stuck up and Kyra was an emotional loudmouth. That's what made their relationship good. They both provided something that the other lacked. Liam provided the level head that Kyra needed, while Kyra helped Liam show some emotions and made him seem like an actual person instead of a walking, talking book. Did they have fights? Yes, what couple doesn't every once in a while? Alright, maybe a little more than once in a while. Fine, they fight a lot, but that's not the point. They still love each other very much. Kyra is just trying to make Liam jealous by flirting with other men. She isn't enjoying it either. She is just doing it for petty reasons. Now Kyra is making them both miserable in the end.*

"Kyra, do you want to get something to drink?" I asked.

Kyra smiled and said, "Sure. Why not?"

As she took the first step away, she suddenly remembered all the men around her. Kyra put on a fake smile and said, "Do pardon us, gentlemen; we are going to go and get something to drink."

Kyra grabbed my hand and pulled me over to where a server was standing holding a tray of drinks. On the tray were long neck glass flutes that were filled with a bubbly yellowish-orange, almost beige liquid with a thin layer of white bubbly foam at the top. The server held the tray out in front of us, and Kyra and I helped ourselves to a glass of champagne. The server then promptly walked away without a second glance at us. I studied the liquid in the glass for a few seconds, while Kyra did not waste any time guzzling it down.

Kyra saw me staring at it and asked, "Is something wrong?"

I continued to look at the bubbly liquid before asking, "What kind of drink is it?" I held it close to my nose as I breathed in something that smelled like fresh fruit.

"It's champagne, Bora," Kyra said, before placing her empty glass on a table nearby.

I took a deep breath as I prepared myself for a conversation with Kyra, not entirely sure how she would react to what I had to say. "Kyra," I said, while swallowing a small lump in my throat before continuing, "I know that Liam hurt you, but that doesn't mean you should hurt him back."

As I continued to talk, Kyra's smile started falling with each of my words. She then said, "I see you are on Liam's side," before backing away.

"No, I am not on anyone's side. I just want you both to be happy."

Kyra then snapped and said, "I'll be happy when Liam is miserable!" She looked around the room, making sure nobody around them had heard what she'd said. Once she confirmed that no one did, she relaxed a little. She pulled me close and whispered into my ear and said, "You know why Liam and I have yet to get married? It is because we both agreed when we were younger, after we told each other that we loved each other, that we would get married, but guess what? Liam never did. He has never said I love you back."

Now I felt very bad for butting in. I said, "Kyra—"

But before I could finish, Kyra said, "Stay out of this. You clearly know nothing about relationships, so stay out of my life and go away."

I walked away without saying another word. In anger, Kyra grabbed the champagne flute sitting on the table, where I had left it, and chugged it down before putting on another fake smile and walking back to the flock of men.

I continued to walk, not sure where to go other than to stay far away from Kyra. That was when I became aware of a strong musty, flowery perfume, and then a smokey and tobacco smell flooded my nose. It was almost overwhelming. I followed the smell and saw three familiar faces: Trista, Theron, and Willow. Trista wore a long tight black dress with black lace sleeves. Her hair was in a braid at the back of her head. Theron wore a very old suit that looked like any wrong move would cause it to rip. Last was Willow. She wore a long forest-green jumpsuit with large gold stems and a leaf necklace, and her dark gray hair was in a matching green turban on her head. As I got closer, I realized that the smell was coming from Trista and Theron who were probably wearing the scent to cover up the smell of alcohol on them. I then remembered what King Maverick had said about Theron finding the hag's dead body.

"Theron," I said.

And he immediately looked at me, irritated and uninterested, and said, "What do you want?"

"Where did you find the hag's body?" I asked.

He looked at me confused and said, "What are you talking about?"

"King Maverick told me you found the hag's dead body," I said, confused.

"What? The hag is dead?" he said. He smiled and said, "It's about time."

I thought to myself, *He did not know the hag was dead. He did not find the hag's body.* I was about to ask Theron again to clarify that he had not found the hag when the royal trumpets started playing. As the sound flooded the room, everyone stopped what they were doing and looked in the direction of the grand stairway.

A short man stepped forward at the top of the stairs and said, "I present His Majesty King Maverick."

King Maverick was wearing a black suit and on his head a silver crown with black onyx gems that were darker than the night. As King Maverick descended the stairs, everyone lined up in two rows across from each other. The king walked in the space between the rows, and as he passed, everyone bowed.

King Maverick then went up on the stage and said, "I want to thank everyone for coming here tonight to celebrate my twentieth jubilee celebration, and it is an honor to be your king."

His speech continued for another ten minutes, but I was not paying attention. I kept thinking, *Why did he lie to me?* At the end of his speech, he ordered the orchestra to play. Theron took out a gold pocket watch from his pocket, gave it a quick look, and put it away.

He stepped forward and said, "May I have the first dance?"

"You want to dance with me?" I said.

"Would you believe it if I told you that you remind me of an old friend and I'm bored?" he said.

I gave Theron a straight face til he finally came clean.

Theron huffed and said, "Fine. King Maverick ordered me and Trista not to drink alcohol for at least one hour after the party started."

"Then why do you two smell like booze now?" I said.

"You see, the keywords in the king's order were 'after the party started,' and for me, it has already started."

Theron held out his hand, and I accepted; after all, I had nothing better to do.

Theron pulled me close and whispered in my ear, "Tonight's the night that really matters, so trust your instinct at all times and remember what Trista told you."

I stared at him and asked, "What do you mean?"

But he refused to speak for the rest of the dance. As we danced, I studied what was going on around us. Kyra was still flirting with several young men in the room, while Liam had a glass in hand giving death glares to all the men standing around Kyra. A few of the men got the hint and slowly backed off. Trista was over at the buffet table looking over it with traumatized eyes. My mind went back to what King Maverick had said about the loss of his sister's sanity. I felt bad, not only for Ann and Trista but for King Maverick as well, particularly since the twins must not be the easiest for King Maverick to handle at times.

Around the room, a small group of women were staring and possibly gossiping about me. The women pointed in my direction and snickered and laughed, making fun of me for my plain yellow dress. Willow was sitting near them with a plate of food in front of her. After a minute or two of listening to their chattering and laughing about me, Willow picked up the napkin that was on her lap and wiped her face with it before placing it on the table and standing up. When she stood up, she pushed in her chair and made her way over to the group of women.

She butted in and said, "Pardon me," while the women were talking.

"Oh, Dragoness Willow, to what do we owe the pleasure?" one of the women asked.

Willow replied, "Class is so hard to find this day, isn't it? You see Ms. Bora over there?" Willow said, pointing in my direction.

Several of the women nodded, and for the first time all night, they were quiet.

Then one of the women spoke up and said, "Isn't she that classless woman from Arm? She has no class, and if she is disturbing you,

I would be happy to tell a guard that she is an intruder. He will get her out of here for you."

Willow became stone faced and said, "Actually, that woman from Arm has more class and grace in her little finger than all of you have in your entire being. I would highly appreciate it if you all kept your mouths shut about her, or else I will have to cut out all of your tongues."

At that moment, all the women went pale and nodded, clearly understanding. Willow turned on her heels and walked back to her seat. When she sat down, she looked me straight in the eye. Her green eyes met my dark brown, and I mouthed thank you to her and Willow nodded back. Theron and I continued to dance for at least an hour until he disappeared to the bar.

I was feeling quite parched from all the dancing, so I went to one of the tables to get a drink for myself. I stood on the side, watching people dance and having fun while holding a glass of water in my hand. I was about to take my first sip when it was slapped out of my hand, breaking into pieces. I turned my head and saw Trista.

She whispered, "Never drink. Never drink," over and over again.

A voice from behind me said, "Excuse me, Trista, Bora, can you come with me? I have something important to talk to you about."

I saw that King Maverick was behind me. Trista looked panicked like she wanted to say something, but she looked like an animal that had been beaten into submission. She gave me pleading eyes, almost begging me not to go.

King Maverick said, "It appears your medicine is wearing off."

He gestured for the guards, and two uniformed men quickly made their way over to him. When they arrived King Maverick said, "It appears my sister's medicine has worn off. Can you escort her back to her room?"

Neither of them said anything. They both grabbed Trista tightly by her upper arm and forcefully walked her away.

Once she was out of sight, I heard a voice beside me say, "That was excessive, don't you think?" I turned to see none other than Theron standing there.

"How did you get here so fast?" I asked.

The last time I saw him, he was making his way to the bar on the other side of the room.

"Ah, Theron, I was just looking for you. I was wondering if you would play a song for all of us. After all, you were considered to be one of the best piano players in the world."

Theron's face hardened as he said, "You know I don't play for audiences anymore."

"Yes, I know, but this is a special occasion. So let's make a deal: you play one song of your choosing, and I will pay you any amount you desire," King Maverick said.

Theron was just about to say something, but was cut off by King Maverick, "It is a real shame, isn't it?"

"What is a shame?" This confused Theron.

King Maverick said, "Oh, just the fact that Willow turned three hundred this year."

Theron's eyes darted to where Willow was sitting as King Maverick continued to speak.

"I heard that when she was younger, she used to dance and have the time of her life while you played the piano. I bet she would love to hear it at least one more time. Don't you agree?"

Theron said nothing. His eyes traveled over to where Willow was sitting and watching the others dancing and having fun. She wanted to join in, but unfortunately, her aching joints did not agree. Willow looked a tad bored but tried to hide it with a small smile on her lips. Her expression was not what I was studying; I noticed every one of her fine lines and wrinkles, her dry rough skin, her dulled and uneven skin tone, and a few age spots. Theron and I stood there a moment looking at her.

Then he pulled his eyes away from Willow and said, unhappily, through gritted teeth, knowing he had lost this one, "Fine, Maverick. You win."

King Maverick chuckled. "Splendid, and it is King Maverick to you, Theron."

Theron was not listening. He just walked away without giving King Maverick or me a second glance. Theron headed directly to where the musicians were playing. As he walked over, people quickly got out of his way as everyone he passed had their eyes on him. Once he reached the stage, he climbed the stairs to join the other musicians. Theron stood on the stage and looked around at all the musicians, who had stopped playing.

The conductor walked over to Theron and asked, "Is there anything in particular you want us to play, Great Dragon Theron?"

Theron's eyes shifted back and forth one last time before landing on the conductor. In an unimpressed tone he said, "No, thank you, gentlemen. I can take it from here."

None of them said anything. They hastily took their instruments and left the stage. Theron walked over to the piano and pulled out the bench. He plopped himself down on it before pulling it in as he placed his hands into position. Theron closed his eyes as he brought his hands down onto the keys and started playing, as if it were as easy as taking a breath of air. He started playing the melancholic song that I had heard him play in Arm. All the guests in the room watched him as his fingers roamed over the keys like it was second nature. Liam smiled as he watched and listened to Theron play. I thought, *Yes, it was public knowledge that Theron used to be famous for being one of the greatest pianists, but no one had heard him play in years. Even the old song Theron was now playing somehow felt far more special than when anyone else played them.*

Kyra stood motionless, as if she had been put in a trance. She could not take her eyes off Theron for even a second; she was so mesmerized with the scene in front of her. Willow closed her eyes, as if hearing Theron play again brought back so many memories to her. I saw tears slowly falling down Willow's cheeks. It was amazing how seeing Theron playing the piano had such an effect on everyone in the room. All eyes were on him and him alone. Theron took a deep breath and continued to play. I stood there watching Theron play for a few minutes when I felt someone tap my shoulder. That was when I remembered King Maverick was standing right by my side. Before I could say anything, King Maverick grabbed my hand and led me away. Everyone was too distracted watching Theron to notice that I was being led away.

He brought me upstairs, straight down a hallway to a terrace. The terrace was large and there was a fast-flowing river below. The full moon was shining brightly in the sky allowing us to see the miles of forest and the lights of the town of Perth not far in the distance.

He leaned on the railing and said, "Enjoying the beautiful view?"

"Very much," I said.

King Maverick said, "I want to apologize for any odd behavior of my sister. She has been sick for a long time, and she doesn't take her psychiatric medicine according to the time schedule. Please sit down, Bora, while I go and get us something to drink."

King Maverick left, and within a few minutes, he returned quickly. "Here you go, Bora."

He handed me a white teacup with the dragon crest on it. The tea smelled similar to orange blossom, but something was off because it also had a slightly pungent smell.

I turned to him and asked, "What kind of tea is this?" I took a small sip of the tea, and it was extremely bitter. The next thing I knew my mouth felt dry and my stomach started to burn.

King Maverick said, "Bora, I haven't been completely honest with you," then briefly paused. "I believe your mother was Queen Sada and she was the love of my life and I miss her every day."

He put his hands on my shoulder. "With you here, I can finally finish my mission, which I have had since the day you were born."

Next thing I knew, he pulled me into a tight embrace. I looked around and wondered what was happening to me. My body started to feel strange.

King Maverick then whispered in my ear. "I forgot to tell you that it was Moon Lilie tea."

I struggled to get out of his grip and pulled away then I felt a slight pain in my chest. I used the last of all my remaining strength and was able to push King Maverick away but only a few feet. I looked down and saw blood coming from my chest staining my yellow dress. It took me a moment to process what had happened. Maverick had poisoned me and then stabbed me in the chest with a knife. The knife was sharp and easily cut through my flesh. Suddenly my mouth was taken over with a taste similar to copper. I opened my mouth slightly, allowing my saliva to roll down my chin like a stream, so I could see what it was. It was extremely warm as I brought my hand up and touched it. I then brought my hand in front of my eye so I could see better. I held my hand out in the bright moonlight and saw a dark stain on my hand. There was a good amount of my blood, and I knew I was in trouble. My vision then started to blur, and I didn't know if it was from the Moon Lilie tea or from being stabbed by King Maverick.

He started talking again while slowly making his way over to me, "I loved your mother; Bora, I truly did, with all my heart, but she betrayed me when she married your father.

"It was a night just like this all those years ago, but you don't remember since you were only a few hours old. Sada died in the exact spot you are standing in now. She had just given birth to you earlier that day and your father was by her side, but I waited for him and as soon as he was alone I killed him. Sada searched the castle looking for him. She was holding you in her arms standing looking over the railing at the water below. I came up behind her and stabbed her in her back with a long sword. Her arms went limp, and you fell into the river below. I pulled out the sword and she turned to me with a small smile and said, 'I forgive you.'"

In less than a moment, King Maverick's straight face was now wearing a big scowl as he calmly said, "I had no choice; she picked that bastard over me."

I was now backing up, having nowhere else to go. I continued to back up until I hit something hard and knew it was the balcony railing. King Maverick was slowly walking closer. I was backed into a corner unable to move. I was starting to black out and was struggling to stay on my feet, let alone keep my one eye on him.

Next thing I knew, King Maverick's face was inches away from mine as he whispered, "I take no pleasure in your death or the death of your family. And say hi to your dad in hell for me," before pushing me off the balcony.

Within seconds, I was descending into the icy cold dark black river below. In a dream-like state, I felt my body floating down the river. Suddenly two figures standing on the riverbank pulled me out of the river.

The smaller one said, "Quickly! She is not dead yet."

That was the last thing I heard before everything went black.

CHAPTER 12

Music, Memories, and Fire

I WAS IN A DARK space. I heard a familiar woman's voice calling for me.

"Hope! Hope, my dear, it is time to get up."

I then felt a hand on my shoulder that was gently shaking me awake. I begrudgingly opened my eyes and saw the outline of a person. I saw Ms. Joy, a beautiful woman who had dark skin, brown eyes, and a shaved head. She wore a long light blue tunic that was tied tightly with a white sash that she used for a belt. She was kneeling down at the side of the bed I was in.

She said, "Hope, come on. You need to get up."

That's right. Hope is my name, not Bora, I thought. Then Ms. Joy stood up and walked over to open the window, causing the sound of the birds to flood into the room. I then sat up in the small bed I was in and started rubbing my eyes. Once Ms. Joy noticed I was up, she left the room telling me to get dressed. I put on a beige dress that looked like it was made with a couple of different fabrics that were all sewn together.

After I was dressed, I noticed that everything seemed so big. I ran over to a long rectangular mirror. The one staring back at me was me when I was five years old. My dark hair was a little longer than my shoulders. I grabbed a hairbrush from a dresser nearby and started to brush my hair. I tied my hair back before running out of my room and down a hallway to the kitchen where I grabbed a slice of bread and a small piece of cheese that Ms. Joy had left for me. Next, I ran through the house and then out of the front door. I ran into the garden that surrounded the house. Surrounding the garden was a tall stone wall that blocked anyone from seeing what was on the other side. I walked around the garden looking to find Ms. Joy. After walking around the side yard, I spotted Ms. Joy picking some tomatoes and then placing them into a brown weaved basket that was sitting on the ground. I ran over to her and stopped behind her.

Then I asked with a wide and bright smile on my face, "Mama, how did I get my name?"

Ms. Joy slowly turned around to me. She spoke softly and said, "Child, I am not your mother, so please do not call me that. You know my name is Ms. Joy." She then cupped my cheek and said,

"Your mother loved you more than life itself. I have no right to be called your mother. Although I love you very much, I did not give you life. As for your name, I had to choose a name for you. Your given name would give you away, and we are keeping you hidden and safe with me. I chose Hope because I have great hope for your future," she said with a wide smile. "Can you please grab the basket, my dear girl?" Ms. Joy said.

I nodded and handed her the basket. She walked over and stopped at the cucumbers and examined them before picking the ones that were ripe. After several hours of harvesting in the garden all different kinds of vegetables, Ms. Joy headed to the tall wooden gate, the gate that led to the outside world.

Ms. Joy noticed I was following close behind her and said, "Hope, my dear, we have been over this so many times—you need to stay here where it is safe. As your guardian, it is my job to make sure you stay hidden."

I then started pouting. Ms. Joy got down on her knees and hugged me. She then said, "I know it is not fair, but for now, you will need to endure it. Soon enough, you will be full grown and ready to leave. Til then, can you be a good girl for me and wait here til I get back? Ok?"

I then felt guilty and shook my head in agreement. Ms. Joy then kissed my cheek and stood back up with the harvested basket of food still in her hand as she then left through the gate before closing it behind her. She often left me alone for hours as she distributed food to those in need. I did not like it when Ms. Joy left. I understood that she was feeding people who were hungry, but I hated being alone with nothing to do.

After Ms. Joy left, I was sitting in the garden with a book that I had read hundreds of times before and I was not that interested in reading it again. That was when a butterfly landed on the page in front of me. The butterfly had white wings that had black tips and two black dots on each. The underside of its wings was pale green. It walked back and forth across the page before it took off flying once again.

When it did, I immediately put the book down and chased after it as it flew through the garden. It stayed high enough out of reach as I followed closely behind. After a while, the butterfly flew over to the garden gate before disappearing over the garden wall and leaving me and the garden behind. I then stood there, disappointed after losing my playmate. That was when I noticed the gate was not fully closed. I pushed the door slightly, and it opened. I looked at the outside world, not sure what I was going to do now, but my mind was immediately made up when I saw the butterfly and I started chasing it again. I ran after it for a long time before getting tired and losing the butterfly. That was when it dawned on me how much trouble I was really in.

I was in a forest with no idea where I was. I then started to cry, but suddenly in the distance, I could hear the sound of music being played. I then ran in the direction of the music and started to slowly follow the sound until I came to its end. I had located the source. It was an old-looking red faded house. The yard was poorly kept with tall weeds and random spots of overgrown grass. I then saw how one of the rooms on the second story had its window open.

I then started to yell, "Hey, excuse me. I'm lost. Can you help me?"

Unfortunately, no one replied; the music just played on. So I yelled louder a couple of more times, but I still got no answer. I then ran over to the front door. When I arrived, I tried to open the door, but it did not budge. I kept pulling on the door handle and calling out, "Hello."

After a while of pulling on the door handle, I tripped and fell, knocking over a bare flowerpot, causing dirt to get all over the front porch and me. I stood up and started to brush the dirt off me. Then I noticed that there was something shiny lying in the dirt. I then reached in and pulled it out. That was when I saw it was a gold key. Curiously, I put the key in the door lock and turned it. When I did, the door immediately unlocked allowing me inside.

Then, I entered the house, and I noticed how dusty it was. The house looked as if it was abandoned. It was almost completely empty except for a few pieces of furniture covered in white sheets. The sound of the music was still playing. It rose and fell and was pulling me toward it as if I had no choice. I followed the sound of the music up the stairs to the second story and down a hallway where the music was so overpowering it was easy to find where it was coming from. I opened the door to a room where the music was and saw a man seated and playing at a piano.

I ran over to him and said, "Hi."

When he saw me, he stopped playing and stared at me. Then he said, "Oh, you're Joy's little thing. What are you doing here?"

I did not say a word.

"Why don't you go back to her? Go on now. Shu shu."

I then hugged the piano leg and said, "I'm lost and I don't know how to get back to Ms. Joy."

"Fantastic," the man said with a huff, before turning back to the piano and continuing to play.

I then let go of the piano leg and climbed onto the piano bench beside him. I turned to the man and asked, "What is your name?"

"My name is Theron," he said.

"My name is Hope," I replied.

"I know who you are. I have known you for a very long time," he said.

I asked, "How come I don't know you? Ms. Joy said I need to be kept hidden to be safe.

Am I safe with you?"

"You are safe with me," he grumbled.

"How do you know how to play music?" I asked.

The man stopped playing again and said, "I play the piano notes from memory of hearing the music previously played. I don't use sheet music."

"Wow, you must be super good at it then," I said.

"I suppose I am," the man said.

"Is playing the piano fun?" I asked.

The man did not look at me. He only stared down at the piano keys and said, "No. I do not enjoy playing it in the slightest."

"Then how come you still play the piano?" I said.

The man was silent for a moment before replying, "I play because it is the only thing I know how to do."

I then started to press a few keys to see what he would do. The man then played the same keys that I did. We continued that for hours where I would play a few keys and he would copy whatever keys I hit.

Eventually, the sound of yelling could be heard in the distance, and as it got closer, I realized it sounded like Ms. Joy. She sounded very upset, and I wanted to run and hide because I knew she was upset because I had not obeyed her and I left the garden. Once she was closer, I could make out what she was screaming.

"Theron! Theron, she is gone and I don't know where she is!"

The voice repeated those words as Ms. Joy ran up the stairs to the room we were in. In the doorway stood Ms. Joy out of breath and staring at me. Ms. Joy then panted out, "How did you open the gate?"

I smiled at her and said, "You didn't close the gate all the way."

She was quiet for a moment before collecting herself and saying, "Come along, Hope. We're going home."

"Ok," I said, before hugging Theron goodbye and saying, "Thanks for playing with me."

Theron did not say anything; he didn't even hug me back. He just looked at Ms. Joy, concerned. Seeing how Theron reacted made her laugh a little, and all he could do was glare at her.

When I finally did let go of him, he said, "Joy, make sure this doesn't ever happen again."

Ms. Joy only chuckled at that and said, "I'll see what I can do."

Unfortunately, for Theron, this was not the last time he would receive an unwanted visitor. To me, it became a sort of game where escaping the garden and visiting Theron was a mission accomplished.

When I was seven, I witnessed cruelty for the first time. I was on my way to Theron's house when I saw some boys who looked a few years older than me. They were throwing rocks and trying to hit a bird sitting high in a tree unaware of the danger it was in. The boys were dirty and wore clothes that were stained. Ms. Joy and I had long come to an agreement that I could go visit Theron on occasion as long as I was not spotted by any of the villagers or Minotaurs.

So I hid in the bushes and just watched the boys. I saw one of the rocks they threw hit the bird and knock the bird out of the tree, and it fell to the ground. Then together, the boys picked up a bigger rock and dropped it on the bird. A loud cracking sound could be heard, and that was when I felt tears start to swell in my eyes. I had to put my hand over my mouth to prevent myself from making any noise.

After a few minutes, the two boys ran off seemingly to find another animal to terrorize. I made sure the coast was clear before running out from behind the bushes to the rock the bird was under. The edges of the rock were uneven and rough. I tried to get it off the bird, but it was extremely heavy, so it took me a while. When I finally moved the rock, I was able to see the bird was flat, surrounded by a pool of blood. I then carefully picked up its limp body. I started to cry as I held the bird close to me and ran to Theron's house.

When I got there, I climbed in through a low window and then ran upstairs to where Theron was playing the piano. When I arrived at the doorway, I was unable to speak and just stood there frozen. Almost immediately, Theron knew I was there. He stopped playing the piano and turned to look at me. His eyes widened at the sight of me in front of him holding a dead bird covered in blood. He did not say anything, so I ran over to him and held out the bird in front of me.

I then asked him, "Can you help this bird?"

After a moment, he stood up and left the room. He then returned with an old wooden cigar box. He knelt down next to me and opened the box. He then signaled for me to put the bird in the box. When I did, he took out a white handkerchief and laid it over the bird. After he did that, Theron placed the lid on the box and closed it.

He then stood up and said, "Go freshen up. If Joy sees you like that, you will give her a scare."

I then looked down at myself and realized how much blood was on my clothing. Then with much irritation in his voice, he said, "Enough delaying now. Go wash up!"

"But what am I supposed to wear? My dress is ruined!" I said.

Theron then went quiet as if he was thinking and said, "I think I have something I can give you to wear."

Theron left the room for a second time and came back carrying a green dress.

I asked, "Why do you have a dress?" It seemed funny to me that a man who lived alone would have a dress in his house.

He simply replied, "It had belonged to an old friend who had left it here long ago. It will be too big for you, but with some string, we'll make it work. I kept it as a reminder of better times that have long since passed now. Just hurry up and go get cleaned up."

After cleaning up, I put on the green dress. I tied the string around my waist tightly, letting the extra fabric hang down over the string to adjust the length of the dress. I looked in the mirror and thought, *Not bad*. Then I walked back into the room with the piano. Theron was sitting on the bench smoking a cigar and looking out into space. The box with the bird was next to him.

"Theron," I yelled, which made him jump, snapping him out of the trance he was in.

He looked at me and said, "Sorry, kid, didn't see you there," while putting his cigar in an ashtray nearby.

I then looked down at the dress and asked, "Whose dress was this?"

"Why do you want to know about a ratty old dress like that?" he said.

I just looked at him with a blank expression on my face.

Theron hesitated before saying, "I had already told you: it belonged to an old friend."

"What happened to your friend?" I asked.

"She is now all grown up and no longer needs it," Theron said.

When Theron said that, there was something in his voice that sounded unfamiliar.

"Do you miss your friend, Theron?"

"Yes and no. Yes, because I am happy to see her grow up, but I am also sad that life back then was much simpler than it is now." All of a sudden, Theron let out a hiss as he gripped his side intensely.

I asked, "Are you ok?"

"Yeah, yeah, I will be fine. Just go get me that bottle on the table over there."

Near the window was a table covered in an old sheet with a tall bottle that held an amber-brown liquid inside. I quickly ran over and grabbed it and brought it over to him. Once I handed it over to him, he did not hesitate before ripping the cap off and starting to chug the amber liquid inside. After a few seconds, he pulled his mouth away from the bottle to take some deep breaths.

When he did, I asked him, "What are you drinking?"

"Whiskey," Theron said out of breath. He had a couple more sips before putting it down and said, "I need this to help with the pain that comes on suddenly and this is the only thing that makes my pain bearable."

I looked at Theron and saw the pain for the first time. It had always been there. I knew Theron was hiding something from me. Now I knew he had been in pain.

I said, "Theron, you are worrying me; I don't want you to be in pain."

Theron started to laugh, but his laughter quickly turned into a coughing fit.

"Oh, Theron, why do you smoke? Don't you know it will kill you?"

Theron then laughed even harder. Looking around, I suddenly noticed that there were several empty bottles scattered around the room.

I then asked, "How often do you drink that stuff?"

He did not look at me when I asked; his eyes were focused on the whiskey in the bottle. He then said, "More often than I should."

"If you drink this stuff so often, then how come this is the first time I've seen you drink it?" I asked.

"I try not to drink around you because Joy says I am setting a bad example for you." Theron then drank whatever was left in the bottle before he put it on the piano to be forgotten about. The rest of the time I was there, we really didn't say anything to each other. I was staring out the window as Theron played the piano. Eventually, Ms. Joy came to get me like she always did.

When she got to the room, she noticed the sadness in the air and asked, "What is wrong?"

Theron then stood up with the small wooden box under his arm and dragged Ms. Joy out of the room. I heard their voices, but I couldn't make out what they were saying. That was when I heard a loud gasp from outside before they both entered again. When they came back inside the room, Ms. Joy thanked Theron for taking care of me before leading me by my hand out of the room. We continued to walk holding hands until we reached home.

Once there, Ms. Joy asked me to find a large rock in the garden, which I ran off to find immediately. When I found her, she was under an apple tree digging a deep hole. I then cleared my voice to get her attention. She asked if I had the rock and I said yes.

"Come here," she said.

Which I did and knelt down next to her. She then put the box in the hole and started to cover it with dirt. She then asked if I was going to help or not. I started to copy what she was doing. When the hole was full of dirt, she then placed the rock over it.

I then asked, "Why?"

Ms. Joy wrapped one of the arms around my shoulder and hugged me. Then Ms. Joy spoke, "Child, the bird has long since passed. It is only right to give it a grave for what it had been through. We bury the dead as a resting place for the body and in honor of a life lived."

For the first time in my short life, I understood the concept of life and death. I then asked, "Do my parents have a resting place?"

Ms. Joy looked at me and with a sad look on her face said, "Yes, they do have a resting place. Someday you will visit that place, and you will bring honor to their lives."

As I Look back on that day, the lessons that Ms. Joy taught me have still stuck with me all these years later.

I was a late bloomer when it came to my special ability. I was around nine when it started happening. Around this time, Ms.

Joy was getting more and more concerned each year that passed. I remember, shortly after my ninth birthday, seeing the black cat for the first time and thinking of him as nothing more than a new friend to play with. Can you imagine how surprised I was when the black cat shifted into a man? He had tan skin and black hair that was just starting to gray. He looked no older than late thirties or early forties.

When he was in his cat form, we would play tag, hide and seek, and I would read to him. When he was in his human form, we would play pretend pirates, which was our favorite game. I remember the day when Ms. Joy and Theron found out. We were all in the garden. I was in the shade of a tree having a tea party with Ryder. Ms. Joy and Theron were sitting on a bench not too far from me watching. I remember listening in on their conversation and being sad over what I heard.

Ms. Joy said, "Thank you for coming, Theron. I know you don't like to get out much. The reason that I. . . I asked you to come here is because I am concerned about Hope."

Theron then rolled his eyes and said, "Not this nonsense again."

Ms. Joy replied, "Yes, this nonsense again! From the books I've read, it is normal for children like Hope to be showing signs of magical abilities at the age of five, and I have yet to see her do anything of the sort!"

Theron then said, "I have two ideas for what is happening. One, she is just a late bloomer, and the other is that the gene pool finally dwindled and she has no magical abilities."

Ms. Joy then exclaimed, "How is that possible? Her father had magic, as did her mother; so she should at least be able to do something, shouldn't she?"

After I had heard what was said, I looked down at my hands, holding back tears. I didn't want to upset Ms. Joy, but I was unsure of what to do. I didn't know any magic. What pulled me out of my thoughts was Ryder asking for sugar in his tea.

I then smiled and said, "Ok, here you go," before putting imaginary sugar cubes into the cup of tea he was drinking from.

Theron glanced at me out of the corner of his eye as a small smile made its way to his lips. He then noticed me talking to someone, and his smile instantly fell.

He then turned to Ms. Joy and asked, "Who is Hope talking to?"

"Probably her imaginary friend," she said.

"How long has she had this imaginary friend for?" Theron asked.

Ms. Joy shrugged and said, "I don't know, maybe a few weeks. Why is that important?"

"I see you are not aware of what is going on here," he said.

"I beg your pardon?" Ms. Joy asked.

Theron then leaned forward and whispered something that I could not hear into her ear. About halfway through his speaking, Ms. Joy's eyes widened unnaturally.

Then Theron pulled away and stood up and said, "It appears you have wasted both of our time. Have a good day." He then stopped at the gate. He smirked and said, "Hope! Tell Ryder I think I have a few rats for him to chase if he ever wants to stop by sometime."

Ryder was in his human form pretending to sip his imaginary tea, gritting his teeth, and yelled, "You wish! You wouldn't even know I was there."

When he yelled it, it was so loud, I covered my ears. When he was done yelling, I uncovered them.

Ryder then said, "Sorry I was too loud. I forget no one can hear me but you."

"Yeah, too loud," I mumbled out.

"My emotions got the best of me. Do you forgive me?"

I smiled and nodded.

Ryder then asked, "Can you repeat what I said to Theron?"

"Ok," and yelled, "Theron, Ryder said he will take care of the rats."

That caused Theron to start laughing while Ms. Joy continued to stare at me, unsure of what to say. Theron then walked out of the garden not even bothering to close the gate door behind him.

I was sixteen. Ms. Joy had told me some details of my parents' death and how they were killed because of jealousy, power, and revenge, that my parents loved each other very much and they were so happy to be having a baby. Ms. Joy refused to tell me the whole story and said when the time is right, she will tell me everything. She put off telling me because she wanted me to have a normal childhood.

"No child deserves to live in constant fear and stress."

After hearing about my parents and how I was cheated from knowing them, I struggled with anger, sometimes taking it out on Ms. Joy. I hated my sixteen-year-old self for that exact reason. I was constantly moody and angry. Ms. Joy had given me a sword to train with.

She said, "You need to get out your anger on something else besides me."

I, unfortunately, was horrible, no matter how much I practiced. I remember training all day when Ms. Joy called me to come in to eat supper. I snapped and yelled at her for no reason, and soon after that she had left. I started feeling horrible for yelling at her.

The argument ended with her saying, "How come you're always so difficult? Your mother wasn't."

That caused me to snap back saying, "Well, I'm not my mother. I will never be her because I have no idea of who she was! I have never seen a picture of her."

Ms. Joy was at a loss for words. She looked at me with pity, and I hated it so much that I stormed off before she could say another word.

I continued to walk the same path that had been embedded into my memories for years until I reached Theron's house. He was sitting on the front step smoking his cigar in his old leather jacket with far too many burn holes in it. I climbed a few steps and sat next to him. He was staring up at the night sky. We both sat there and stared up at the starry sky, and neither of us said a word. We sat in silence, and I found myself for the first time in a long time feeling peaceful inside. The moon was shining brightly and illuminated everywhere as far as the eye could see. We did not talk, but every once in a while, my eyes would drift over to Theron. He was sitting with one of his knees against his chest while the other was laid out straight in front of him.

Every so often, the breeze would carry the ashes from his cigar and glowing tinder would float far away into the nighttime sky.

Theron finally spoke, "So when are you going to go back and apologize?"

When he said that, I was completely taken back. I snapped and said, "I'm not my mother."

Theron shrugged and said, "I never claimed you were. This world is hard. No one has it easy. Children can't pick who they're born to or the consequences that come with being who they are. At the end of the day, you, Hope, need to decide who you want to be. It is your decision that falls solely on you. You decide the life you want to live. You cannot blame others for your actions or your

choices. So let me ask you who you want to be."

I remained silent, and that was when I noticed Ryder was in his cat form sitting in front of me giving me a look saying, "You know he's right."

"I have something for you," Theron said, before shifting to his other side to grab something that was next to him. Once he held it in his hands, I was able to see—it was a long metal staff.

I jokingly said, "What am I going to do with that, beat someone like a rug?"

He continued to hold it out in front of me until I took it away from him. In my hand, the staff started to transform, and it turned into a scythe.

"Why are you giving this to me?"

"Joy said you are having trouble with the sword she gave you. I think this may be a better fit for you." He continued, "And by the way, you're welcome."

I stared at it and ran my fingers over the side of the blade, mesmerized by it.

Theron then said, as he was taking another puff of his cigar, "Unlike swords, you use both hands and your upper body. You need to use swinging motions instead of cutting and jabbing. It is also a lot more inconspicuous to have, in your presence, a staff."

I then started swinging it trying to get a feel for it and accidentally grazed Theron's hand. As soon as that happened, I immediately put the scythe down and reached for Theron's hand that I cut.

Theron pulled his arm away and said, "Don't worry; I am fine."

"Why do you always have to be such a stubborn man?" I said.

As I started looking over his hand where the cut would be, it wasn't there. I noticed there were old scars but nothing new. I continued to look over his hand as it made no sense to me. Eventually, Theron tugged his hand out of my grasp leaving me there questioning what had happened. Theron answered my question before I even needed to ask it. He took off his jacket before rolling up his sleeves. He then took out a pocketknife and plunged it into the underside of his forearm.

I shouted, "What are you doing?"

He then pulled the knife out of his arm. Just as quickly as the knife was pulled from the open cut, it disappeared right before my eyes as if the cut was never there. Theron then said, "It's part of my curse; my body is able to heal at a rampant speed, and the scars heal but underneath are the open wounds."

"I wish I had healing powers like you," I mumbled.

"I don't control the healing. It just happens as soon as I am hurt, and I am unable to stop it even if I wanted to," Theron said.

"How did you get your curse anyway?" I asked.

"I simply broke the laws of time. That is not important. You still are young. We are not even sure what you are capable of. It takes a long time to get a hang of them, and from a young age, you were able to see those who were no longer with us."

"The only dead person I have ever seen is Ryder—I mean Dad. You know what I mean."

"Still can't handle calling him Dad?" Theron chuckled.

"I wish I could see my mom," I said.

"She would be here if she could. Trust me; she wanted you more than anything. You know, unlike your mom, watching you is quite entertaining," he said.

We continued to talk for the rest of the night. When the morning sun started to rise, we said our goodbyes, and I headed home. When I arrived home, I went straight to Ms. Joy's room and apologized for my behavior.

Over the next couple of years leading up to my nineteenth birthday, our relationship got much better to the point where I would consider Ms. Joy my best friend. Unfortunately for me, she seemed to be aging much faster. She was having a harder time maintaining the garden, so I helped out more along with cooking and all of the housework. She still insisted that I needed to be kept a secret, so she continued to carry the fruits and vegetables to the village daily.

Then one night, shortly after my nineteenth birthday, my life would change forever.

I was out in the garden pulling weeds when Ms. Joy came up behind me and said, "We are going to be getting a visitor later. I want you to stay inside and stay hidden. If things go wrong, I want you to run away and leave me behind. Do you understand?"

I looked at her and said, "What? No, of course, I'm not leaving you. You need to tell me who is coming to visit, and why do I need to hide?"

But before I could finish, she said once again, "Do you understand?" But this time, it was more of a statement than an actual question.

I then went quiet and nodded my head.

Later that evening, before the sun completely set, I hid myself away in my bedroom closet. It was dusty and cramped, but I remembered the instructions that Ms. Joy gave me and stayed put. Before going in, I put on a white nightgown thinking, worst-case scenario, I would have to sleep there. Unfortunately for me, I was completely wrong. Shortly after going into the closet, I drifted off to sleep.

Later, I was awakened by the smell of smoke that was suffocating me. I pushed the closet door open to see my childhood room engulfed in flames. I was hardly able to see anything with all the smoke and fire. I ran through the house calling for Ms. Joy and choking on the smoke. Somehow, I found my way out, and our home was now fully overtaken with fire.

I ran through the garden, which was also burning, and remembered Ms. Joy's words as I continued to run. I ran out of the garden gate into the forest. I don't remember how long I ran for, but I do know that, as I ran, my nightgown was getting caught on thorns and branches. I could hear it rip and tangle as I ran through the dark forest. In my panicked state, I lost my way and no longer knew where I was. There was no moon to guide me; only pitch darkness lay ahead. The last thing I remember was my right foot being tangled and falling hard to the forest floor.

CHAPTER 13

Wide Awake

I SLOWLY OPENED MY EYES, and I looked at the room around me. I was in a small stone cabin, far less nice than the one I grew up in. I could tell it was nighttime by the color of the black sky out of the window. I struggled to sit up to get a better view of where I was but felt a sharp pain in my chest causing me to flinch and lie back down. I was trying to think how I got there when the door opened. A small light from a candle slipped in the room, illuminating the small cottage. After a moment, I realized it was Willow. It took me a moment to recognize her because she hardly looked like she once did. She looked unkempt and tired and frail. She looked at me with wide eyes. She let out a noise that sounded like a surprised yelp.

She said, "You're awake?"

I tried to reply, but my throat was so dry I was unable to speak. I tried sitting up again, but she ran over and forcefully pushed my shoulders down.

Willow then said, "I'll go get you some water."

She quickly came back with a glass of water in her hand, which she handed to me with a relieved smile on her face. "Drink it slowly," she advised.

Once I was done drinking, I still struggled to speak and I asked, "Where am I?"

"You're in Bartrex, one of my territories," Willow said.

My voice was shaking as I asked, "How did I get here?"

Willow took my hand, smiled, and said, "Theron had a vision that you were in danger. He saved your life."

She continued. "While Theron was playing the piano, at the jubilee he had a vision of you. He quickly ended his performance and asked Liam and Kyara to find you. Liam and Kyra searched the castle and reported back to Theron and I. They advised that they could not locate you. Theron then headed toward one of the back doors of the castle. Unfortunately, Theron was still having side effects from the vision and was moving extremely slowly. He was about halfway to the back door when I caught up with him and asked, 'Theron, what do you think you're doing? Bora is missing; we don't want you to

disappear as well!'

"Theron did not say anything. Instead, he opened the door and walked out. I continued to follow behind him and said, 'I suppose some fresh air will be good for you.'

"We continued to walk together; Theron walked ahead of me. We walked through the garden and down to the river to where the water was rushing down the riverbank. Once there, Theron threw off the jacket he was wearing and started rolling up his pants. I asked, 'What are you doing?'

"Instead of replying, he took off his golden pocket watch and put it in my hand. Theron then slid down the riverbank and walked along the riverbank searching for something. We saw a flash. I did not know what it was or what Theron was looking for. I yelled, 'Look,' and then we both just stood there in silence before something came floating down the river.

"Once it came close enough, Theron reached out and grabbed a dark shadow and held it tightly in his arms. I then studied what he had picked up, and it looked to be a body. With the added weight of it and Theron's weakened condition, Theron was slowly losing his footing and struggling to stay upright against the rushing current. 'Quick she is not dead yet,' he said.

"He held out one of his arms signaling for me to help him out of the river. Theron then laid you along the riverbank. He said, "'Looks like we found Bora.'

"You looked extremely pale. We could see blood soaking through your yellow dress. Theron ripped your dress above your chest and found a large laceration. I then said, 'We need to go get help!'

"I turned and started to head back to the castle; Theron grabbed onto my wrist and said, 'If you go in there and tell any of them what you just witnessed, you will be signing Bora's death certificate. Do you understand me?'

"'Yes, I understand,' I said.

"'Now here is what I want you to do. You are going to go in there and tell Liam that I passed out, and we will be leaving immediately so you can monitor me. Once you come back, you will be taking us straight to Bartrex where we can ensure Bora recovers. Understand?'

"I agreed before heading to the castle. Once inside, not everything went as I expected. Getting inside and locating Liam was easy enough, but what Theron did not account for was King Maverick. When I was done talking to Liam, I noticed King Maverick walking toward me. As he got closer, I took a deep breath in and out as I calmed myself, and I put a smile on my face.

"King Maverick spoke first and asked, 'Any news on Bora's location?'

"'Sadly no. Still nothing,' Liam said. 'Willow just came over to inform me of her and Theron's departure.'

"'Oh really? But the night is still young! What reason would the both of you have for leaving, especially while Bora is missing?'

"'Theron has had too much to drink and is not feeling very well, so I am taking him to a friend's so I can monitor him,' I told him.

"'You are more than welcome to use the castle infirmary.'

"'Thank you, but we both know that Theron would be angry if he woke up in the castle infirmary.' I added, 'I am afraid Theron overdid it on the liquid courage. You know he hates playing the piano in public. Theron's aftermath is especially bad; I am worried he is falling ill. The last thing I would want is for you to get sick, Your Majesty. It is easier to move him away, don't you agree?'

"King Maverick fell silent before smiling and saying, 'Very well. I shall not hold you up any longer.'

"I then said my goodbyes, walking away slowly while still in sight of King Maverick. Then I hurriedly got outside and ran back in the direction of you and Theron. When I got back to you, you were looking paler than before. Theron had put a handkerchief in your mouth. He was sitting in the grass next to you with a dagger in his hand. He was using a lighter and was heating up a dagger blade. I asked, 'Theron, what are you doing?'

"Theron did not look at me, but instead, he said, 'I am saving her life!'

"He pressed the hot dagger into where your open wound was. You let out a low-pitched scream that was muffled by the handkerchief in your mouth. I looked at Theron in horror at what he had just done. 'Theron, couldn't you have used your powers?'

"Theron replied, 'I tried, but my powers are still too weak. I did what I had to do.'

"I whispered, 'You cauterized her. On top of that, there could be damage to her heart, and you just closed the wound!'

"Theron then calmly said, 'It was either that or have her bleed out to death in my arms. So if you're asking me, I think I made the right choice.'

"Shortly after that, I shifted into my dragon form, and I carried you and Theron back here. That is what happened, that is how you got here," Willow said.

"Thank you for saving me," I said, with a shaky voice.

Willow then said, "You should not be thanking me, especially since all this is my fault."

I gave her a concerned look and asked, "What do you mean?"

Willow then said, "Your mother Sada was a very self-sufficient woman and refused to accept help anyone. Being queen is a lot harder than you think. Over time, as her work kept piling up because she wanted to do the best for her people, her and your father's relationship became strained. Your father was supposed to sail away on a trip. Maverick saw this as a chance to get rid of him. He then sank the ship with a storm killing all aboard.

"Thankfully, your father did not get on the ship earlier that day because your mother collapsed from exhaustion. This was before your father was to leave the castle, so he insisted on staying with her to make sure she was alright. Later it was found that she was with child, and Sada was forced to take bed rest. Over the months, she and your father reconnected, and their relationship became stronger than ever. Maverick was furious his plan had failed, and with the news of you, he was jealous, dangerous, and desperate—one of the worst combinations out there.

"At the time, I was helping Trista to care for Ann. Since it was not unusual for a brother to check on his younger sisters, I thought nothing of it when Maverick came to visit out of the blue. I was staying with the sisters in their house. One night, he poisoned our food, which caused us to black out, before locking Trista and I in the basement. Ann was locked in the attic. He refused to let us out and would withhold food for days at a time. He threatened to hurt Ann and Trista unless I agreed to help him with his plan."

My mind thought back to what King Maverick had said over tea about Trista's mind being poisoned.

My thoughts were cut off as Willow continued to speak, "After a few months, I gave in for Trista's and Ann's sake. He made me lie about a fast-spreading disease that eventually led to a lockdown. All the castle staff were sent home to take care of their families near the end of Queen Sada's pregnancy.

"Then on April 18, the day you were born, I was the one who had delivered you. At this time, Maverick still had his sisters locked up, so I left to go check on them. After I left, Maverick came to the castle. Your father confronted him and wanted to know why he was there. I don't know what Maverick said to your father, but they fought and your father was killed. Your mother heard the noises and went out to see what was going on. She saw your father get killed, and you know the rest."

I then asked, "How come she just didn't shift into her dragon form and escape?"

Willow said, "It is because of her weakened state that she was unable to shift into her dragon form."

"How long was I out anyway?" I asked.

Willow replied, "Three and a half weeks."

"Three weeks!" I yelled in surprise.

"Three weeks, and keep your voice down. Some people are sleeping; it is very late," she said.

"Where is Nessa and the others? Are they alright?" I asked.

Willow nodded and said, "Yeah. They're staying here at the moment. Do you have any pain?"

"Yes, in my chest where I was stabbed," I said.

Willow replied, "That is to be expected. Now get some rest; you're still not out of the blue yet."

After that, Willow left the cabin. I looked out the window and saw the bright crescent moon in the sky. Then I noticed the black cat, Ryder, sitting on the windowsill.

We stared at each other for a moment before I said, "Hi, Dad."

Ryder then shifted into his human form and gave me a small smile. He said, "Hey, kiddo."

I then asked, "Why?"

Ryder tilted his head to the side like he had done so many times before and said, "Why what?"

"Why did you not reveal yourself to me? Why did you pretend to just to be a cat?" I said. "I did what I thought was best. Can you imagine what would happen if I came up to you when you first woke up under the willow tree and said, 'Hi I am your dad, and by the way, I am also dead. On top of that, you have a special gift that allows you to see the deceased. Oh by the way, you also have to overthrow the king of this land to take your rightful place as queen.'

"Instead, I led you to someone who I knew would take care of you and constantly did everything in my power to keep you safe!"

Without thinking I said, "I am not sure how deeply you thought out this plan. You do realize I lost an eye, got poisoned, stabbed, and almost drowned."

Ryder looked hurt before turning his back to me and said, "Hope you get better soon," before turning back into a cat and passing through the open window.

Then I lay there alone and felt the waves of regret wash over me. I shouldn't have said that to him. I did not know for how long I stared at the ceiling before I was finally able to drift off to sleep. I was awoken by a bright light. I squeezed my eye shut trying to block out the light but failed. I eventually begrudgingly opened it and saw none other than Theron sitting beside me on a chair. There was no cigar in sight, and the only bottle of whiskey was unopened on the bedside table next to a small shot glass.

"Good to see you awake," he said.

"It's good to be here. Theron, I owe you my life," I said.

Theron said, "I just wanted to see you. How's your chest, by the way?"

"Sore," I mumbled.

Theron then pulled up the bottom half of one side of his shirt and said, "I win."

It took me a moment to realize what I was looking at was part of Theron's skin. The skin there was black and decayed. His skin was so thin you could make out all the different muscles and tendons just by looking at it. It was so horrible, but at the same time, I was unable to look away.

Theron then pulled his shirt down, hiding it, and said, "That's what is known as the beauty of the grotesque, something so hideous and ugly that it captivates all who see it."

"How did you get it?" I asked.

Theron did not look at me. Instead, his eyes lay on the whiskey bottle as he said, "I broke the Rules of Time, so I was cursed. It's that simple."

He then poured some of the whiskey into the shot glasses before pushing it my way. I hesitated before picking it up, but once I did, Theron lifted the bottle up in the air almost like a silent toast. I copied what he did as we locked eyes with each other before he took a drink. I studied the liquid in my glass before taking a sip as well. My eyes watered as the smokey flavor spread through my taste buds before burning the back of my throat. After swallowing the little I had, I placed the shot glass back on the nightstand.

Theron then said, "I overheard some of what you were talking about with Ryder."

I then said, "You're not off the hook either!" He then chuckled as I asked, "What was so funny?"

"You really are nothing like your mother. Other than her eyes— well in

your case it is just eye—you are completely different."

"What do you mean?" I asked.

"She was blander than water. If the places were switched right now, she would have just forgiven me off the bat. You, on the other hand, are a spitfire and far more entertaining.

Also, I should be the one upset that you missed my birthday," he said before bringing the bottle back to his lips.

"Theron I need to know who the hag is and why she was out to hurt me. She once said that I was payback. So I need to know: who was the hag to you?"

"You're right," Theron said. "I should tell you why the hag was after you. It was because of me. Her name was Bonnie."

Theron continued, "Bonnie was an annoying woman who was constantly throwing herself on any good-looking man that caught her eye. Once the War Against Dragons started, Pricilla and I went into hiding. We moved to the large city of Josay to try and blend in. There we met Willow and Oak who were young children. Their parents were sent to the colosseum to die in the arena. We found them one day hiding in the forest and brought them home to live with us.

"Due to Priscilla and I growing up playing musical instruments, we became traveling musicians. We were so good, we often played at nobles' parties. Along the way to one of the locations, we stumbled upon Bonnie who was being attacked by a wild boar, so we saved her. She was about the same age as Pricilla. Pricilla and Bonnie shared the same dreams of marriage and talked endlessly of having children. They even went so far to name all their future children.

"We never told her that we were dragons, but she must have eventually figured it out. Bonnie brought armed guards to our home and revealed we were dragons. Willow and Oak were able to escape through an open window. Pricilla and I were locked up and sent to the colosseum. Pricilla was heartbroken because she had loved and trusted Bonnie. Pricilla died a horrible death in the arena, and I went mad. I tried to save her but ended up killing everyone in the colosseum. After that they ended the War Against Dragons.

"Later, I found Bonnie and used time to turn her into an old woman, to prevent her from ever marrying and having children. Then with the help of a witch, a curse was used to prolong her life."

I was about to say something to him, but Willow beat me to it.

She pushed the door open and said, "There you are, Theron. I've been looking everywhere for you because mysteriously all the alcohol had disappeared and now I find you here bothering my patient no less."

Theron then pulled the bottle away and hid it behind his back. "I was just leaving," he said. But he didn't move.

"Now," Willow said.

Theron stood and headed for the door, but before he reached it, he turned around and said, "Welcome back to the land of the living." Then he was gone.

Once again, I was left alone to my thoughts, and perhaps I should have stayed asleep a little longer as I already felt a headache coming on.

Some hours later, after Willow had fed me, I felt well enough to get some fresh air. As I stumbled to my feet and walked out of the cabin door breathing in the clean morning air, sitting on a circle of logs was my makeshift family. I walked over and took a seat next to Nessa and Avery. Nessa was looking half asleep while drinking something that was undeniably coffee. Avery looked wide awake holding

Kat in her arms and feeding her applesauce. When I sat down next to them, it took a moment for everyone to process that I was there.

"Bora, we are so happy to see you awake. Willow had forbidden us to come and see you this morning. She had told us you were awake. We were sitting here hoping we would see you."

Avery and Nessa both jumped up and rushed over to hug me.

"Good morning, Bora," Amos said with a big smile on his face.

Avery had set Kat down before coming over to hug me. Kat was all smiles and seemed to have once again aged right before my eye.

Nessa was the first one to ask, "How are you feeling, my dear? Shouldn't you be resting?"

"I feel well enough. I needed to get out of that bed and I wanted to see that you all were alright," I said.

Kat then made grabby hands toward me, so I picked her up and held her close to me. When I did, she said something that was unexpected.

Kat said, "Mama."

I looked at the others and asked, "When did she start talking?"

"About a week after the jubilee," Nessa said. "She is also walking now as well."

As she was talking, I looked down studying the young toddler in my arms. She was so big now, I hardly recognized her. Her once dark blue eyes were now a deep brown. Her once bald head now had dark brownish wisps of hair on it. As she opened her mouth, I was able to see a few teeth. She wore a light pink dress and was barefoot.

I smiled wider at her as she continued to hold on to me and say, "Mama," gripping hard on the sleeping gown I was wearing.

At this, Avery seemed a little annoyed yet just as happy as everyone else there.

After a few moments, "What are we going to do now?" Amos asked.

I had no idea what to say as Willow cut in and said, "Whatever you do, you can't stay here forever, and in all actuality, the sooner you all leave, the better because of how close this place is to the castle."

Then all the eyes were on me waiting for me to say something. I had no idea at all about what we should do next. I did not know what to say, so instead I asked, "Where is Theron?"

"He went back to the small house he is staying in after he went to see you," Willow said.

"Where is it?" I asked.

"It is the one straight down the path with the mossy roof. Why?" Willow asked, as she pointed down the path.

"It's nothing," I said. "I just need to talk to him really quick that's all," and handed Kat back to Avery. I quickly got up and walked away.

All the thoughts rushing through my head were driving me crazy. *What are we going to do now? It's my fault for dragging everyone into this situation. What if I pick the wrong option, and it gets them all killed?* That was when a hand was placed on my shoulder, pushing me out of my thoughts. I flinched back and knocked the hand away to see none other than Theron standing there.

Theron said, "Follow me," as he walked away.

We walked a short distance through soft grass until we reached the top of a small hill where Theron plopped himself down on the grass. I followed soon after. He then pulled out a cigar and rifled around in his pockets for, no doubt, a lighter. Eventually, out of frustration he just took the cigar out of his mouth and put it back in his coat pocket.

He mumbled out loud, "Damn Willow is always hiding my things! Are you going to say something, or just sit there like a rock?"

I swallowed before saying, "I need advice."

Theron then laughed, "You are the second person to ever ask me for advice."

"Who was the first?" I asked.

Theron then said, "Joy. She asked me how she should someday tell you about your past. I had no idea; how was I supposed to know?"

"Theron, I didn't even get to say goodbye to Ms. Joy. I know she is gone; I felt it. She was so good to me, she was the mother that I never had. I loved her so very much. How did she die?"

"She was a good woman."

Theron continued, "I buried her in the garden next to the apple tree. I do know she died in the fire, but I don't know if the fire was an accident or if it had been purposely set. I didn't see the fire in my visions, but you can bet that, if it was purposely set, Maverick had something to do with it."

"Thank you, for taking care of her," I said. I then cleared my throat and asked, "What should I do now?"

Theron said, "Whatever you want."

"Not helping," I said.

"Bora, or Hope, whatever the hell you want to be called," Theron said. "I have no idea what you need to do. I can't tell you to put your life in danger and go after Maverick. He is strong. He is much stronger than I am. You haven't even transformed as of yet. You don't have a chance going after him now. You need to wait. Maverick thinks you are dead. He needs to keep thinking that you are for your own safety."

"Ok, I get it," I said. "I need to give it some more thought. I will let you know what I am doing when I figure it out." After a short pause, I said, "I think I am going to go with Bora. I don't even know who Hope was anymore. I think Bora seems to be a better fit for me at least for now."

"Thanks for letting me know," he said. "I will try to remember. I don't know how many times—when you couldn't remember who you were—I almost called you Hope. I think Bora is a perfect fit for you since your mother was a wind dragoness. As of right now, you have time to decide. Don't make any rash decisions. My life is full of regrets more than I could count, so it is better to do what your gut tells you than your own head. Do you get it?"

"Yeah, I think so. Thanks," I said. "Can I ask you one more question, Theron?"

"What now?"

"Why do you still smoke?"

"I smoke because the smell reminds me of a better time in my life. I am not afraid of death; I actually am looking forward to it."

When Theron said that, his eyes looked distant as if he was hundreds of miles away with no interest for the present day. What pulled us both out of our thoughts was the sound of giggling and a young child screaming, "Mama!"

It was none other than Avery with Kat in her arms.

"Avery, what are you doing here?" I asked.

"There is a lake around here, and I thought I might as well go swimming with Kat," Avery said.

Theron then got up and started walking away, saying, "I'm going to go find a light," leaving the three of us alone.

It was silent and awkward for a few minutes before Avery asked, "Do you want to come with us?"

I nodded and followed after her. We walked for a while until we reached a small waterfall that led into a small clear lake. I watched as she took off her boots and socks and climbed into the water wearing shorts and a T-shirt. She held Kat tightly in her arms as Kat squirmed at the touch of the cool water. I would have joined her, but there was a heaviness sneaking in, so I just sat on the shore watching. After a while, she climbed out of the water and sat next to me and rested her head on my shoulder.

"Everything feels so different now," I said. "I finally remembered my past!" I paused after that to see her reaction.

Avery then hesitated and said, "Yeah, Nessa, Amos, and I know as well."

"Who told you?" I asked.

"Theron told us not long after we came here," Avery said. "Any ideas on what we are going to do now?"

I swallowed the lump in my throat and nodded no, not meeting her eyes.

"Well, since I know about your past, I might as well tell you about mine and Amos' past," she said.

I cut her off by saying, "You don't have to if you're not comfortable."

She smiled softly at me and said, "It's fine. I want to tell you, and I promised anyway. I don't know the whole story, but my mother was a noble. She was arranged to be married, but she was in love with someone else. So she and my father, a gardener, ran away together. They came up with the great idea to use the little savings they had to buy a small farm. We were happy on our little farm.

"When we were nine, our mom got tuberculosis, and we were kicked out of the house to go sleep with the animals in the barn because it was contagious. Our father stayed with her to take care of her. Shortly after, our father got it as well, and then they both died. We lost the farm due to taxes, and the new owners let us stay on to work and we continued to live in the barn.

"Eventually, we left due to the new owners not knowing how to run a farm. Amos and I would go to bed hungry almost every night. So we left, and after that, we had to steal to stay alive."

"I am sorry that happened to you and Amos. It must have been hard not having anyone to look after you," I said.

"It wasn't good," Avery said, "but we always had each other. There were so many times Amos went without eating because he always put me first. It's funny how you forget those times in the heat of the moment."

We both heard soft snoring as we looked down in Avery's arms to see a peacefully sleeping Kat. I then looked back down to where we came from to see smoke rising miles away.

"What's that over there?" I asked.

Avery replied, "That is the town for Bartrex. We are staying in the chlorite cabins far away from it to try and hide you from being seen."

"So what exactly did I miss?" I asked.

Avery and I stayed there and talked for hours. She told me how worried they all were about me and how Theron had been the one to tell all of them what had happened, how Willow had invited them all to stay while she took care of me, how they all took turns sitting at my bedside each night, how Willow had insured them they all would be safe there, and how they managed without me.

Around noon, we headed back through the lush green forest to the little spot in the forest where we were staying. My chest started throbbing. I was interested in talking to Willow. Avery told me what cabin Willow lived in, and I headed there while she got Kat fed. The cabin seemed older than all the others from the chipping paint and the mossy roof. I walked up the stone steps to the sun-bleached door and knocked. There was no answer, so I knocked again.

When I did, I noticed the door handle jiggling and turned it, surprised that it was unlocked. As I looked inside, I noticed it was slightly bigger inside than the others. There was an old unmade bed with a pile of knitted blankets sitting at the end of the bed. Next to it was a wardrobe that was very narrow. On the other side was a small kitchen that was next to a fireplace, making up for the fact that it did not have an iron stove. On the fireplace mantel were a number of books, all old and brittle. Next to the fireplace slept a small gray cat.

In the middle of the room sat probably the nicest thing in there: a dark wood desk. The desk was covered in paperwork. As I walked around to get a better look at it, I noticed there were two top drawers and opened the one on the right side. There were some quills and ink along with an old photo. As I looked at the photo, I realized the man in it looked similar to one boy in Theron's photographs. The only difference was that he was all grown up now. In the photo, his smile was so wide that his eyes were almost shut. There were a few scars and bruises on his face, and his chin was covered in whiskers. He also appeared to be well built with broad shoulders.

"What are you doing here?" a voice said.

I looked up to see Willow standing in the doorway. She looked tired and out of breath.

"Sorry. The door wasn't locked, and my curiosity got the best of me!" I said.

"It's fine. The lock on the door is broken anyway," Willow replied.

"Who is the man in the photo?" I asked.

Willow walked over and stated, "It is a photo of my brother Oak. It was taken a few years before he passed. He was a soldier, and if you look next to where the photo was, you will see the letter I received telling me of his demise. Unfortunately he died a hero! In the letter it said that he had been killed, stalling enemy troops, allowing his own troops to escape." She finished by saying, "He was a great man and my best friend."

"I am so sorry for your loss, Willow. He truly died a hero. I understand how we really never get over the loss of our loved ones," I said.

"What can I help you with?" Willow asked.

"I just wanted to ask when it would be ok for me to leave," I said.

"Bora, next Sunday is the earliest, but it is entirely dependent on how you feel."

"I am feeling perfectly fine," I said, while lying through my teeth.

I was putting all of them in danger the longer I stayed with them. So my reasoning was, the sooner I leave, the safer they will all be, or at least that was what I believe.

Willow studied me for a moment before saying, "Splendid. If you continue to feel that way, then you should be on schedule to leave soon. Do you know where you are going to go next?" she asked.

"No, I have no idea at this time, but I need to start making plans," I said.

"Bora, one more thing before you leave," Willow said, stopping me in my tracks. She then went to the other side of her desk, opened the drawer, and said, "I think this belongs to you," while holding up the adder stone.

My eye widened looking at it as the images of the hag and Maverick flashed through my mind.

"The night of the jubilee, King Maverick must have thrown this in the river. Theron went back a few days later and found it. I'm looking for a way to reverse the spell and get your eye back to you," she said.

"Oh, thank you, Willow. I would love to get my eye back to where it belongs," I said before leaving.

My thoughts were now racing through my mind. The last thing I wanted was to put any of them in danger. I needed to leave alone. So I would have to leave at night. That way I would have enough time to leave without any of them noticing I was gone. I was so lost in thoughts that I did not realize that I walked right into someone. I looked up and saw it was Amos.

"Hi, Bora. Lunch is almost ready, so I am just rounding everyone up to eat," he said.

"That sounds amazing. I will be right there," I said.

"Ok. See you at lunch," Amos said cheerfully, before walking away carrying a few pieces of firewood in his hands.

When I got back to my cabin, I noticed just how small it really was. The bed took up most of it, while the side tables hugged the wall leaving little to no room. The bathroom was no better. The white tub was about half my size, and it seemed to have seen better days. I turned on the waterspout, and water sprayed out every which way, getting me soaked. I took a quick bath before lunch. The last time I remembered taking a bath was weeks ago before heading to the jubilee celebration.

When I got out of the tub, I looked in the mirror and almost didn't recognize who was staring back at me. My face was much thinner than it used to be. My hair was wild and matted and looked as if it had not been brushed in weeks. There were bags under my eyes, and I looked paler than I ever had in my life. There was no way I was going to get all the knots out of my hair. I looked in the medicine cabinet for anything to help me. What caught my eye was a thin long metal blade used for shaving. I decided then it was time for a haircut. Quickly I cut away at my hair, dropping it in a pile in the sink. My long hair that once hung to my middle back was now just above my shoulders. I found clean clothes on one of the side tables next to the bed. They were big but clean, so I didn't care.

CHAPTER 14

The Danger I Bring

I WALKED UP TO THE campfire to join the others for lunch. Avery and Amos were bickering over the soup because Amos had put some mushrooms in it while Avery hated mushrooms. Nessa was attempting to get Kat to walk. Kyra was now sitting there far too amused for her own good.

"What kind of soup is it?" I asked.

"It's minestrone," Nessa said, as she continued to try and get Kat to walk.

Amos' eyes drifted over to me as he yelled, "What did you do to your hair?"

"My hair was so tangled I was never going to get the knots out, so I cut it," I said. "It actually feels good not to be weighed down by all my hair. Does it look bad?" I asked.

Everyone was quiet before Avery replied, "No, it looks good. We are just not used to seeing you with short hair."

"Well, I like it," I said.

Nessa broke the silence by saying, "You look good with short hair. You can always grow your hair back if you want to."

Avery yelled, "Nessa is right. You look good."

"Better than good," said Amos.

Kyra nodded her head and gave a thumbs up.

"Lunch is served. That's enough talking. Let's eat," Amos said.

"Kyra, when did you get here?" I asked.

Kyra replied, "I've been staying here ever since Liam and I broke up. You didn't see me this morning because I was busy."

"Busy sleeping in," Avery said.

Kyra snapped back and said, "Fine; you caught me. I'm not an early bird, so sue me!"

We then all sat there and ate in silence. I ate slowly and stared into the orangey red broth and just thought how much I was going to miss all of them. What got me out of my thoughts was Avery complaining about how there was too much Worcestershire sauce in it.

Amos argued back, "The chef doesn't take criticism from people who can't even boil water."

I cut in and said, "It tastes great to me. Thank you."

He threw a smug grin at Avery as she said, "Yes, thank you, Amos, for making lunch, but I would have preferred no mushrooms."

Nessa laughed and said, "There is nothing like the banter of siblings."

"I am your older brother and your twin. I was brought into this world with you, and I will be leaving it with you whether you like it or not."

"Aww, Amos, that's so sweet," I said.

Amos looked confused and asked, "How is it sweet? I'm just scared of dying alone."

At that, Kyra cracked up laughing while Nessa almost spit out her food trying not to laugh.

"And the sibling bonding moment is over," Avery said.

Krya then turned her attention to me and said, "So your mother was a queen and you're a dragon?"

At that, everyone went quiet.

"So it seems," I said.

"Do you know how to shift?" Kyra asked.

"No. I was told very little about my identity, and I know even less about any powers or even the extent of them," I said.

"Don't worry; I can help you," Krya said excitedly.

"It can't be that hard, right?" I asked.

"Are you sure you want to do that, Kyra?" Avery said.

"Why shouldn't I? Do you think I'll be a bad teacher or something?" Kyra snapped.

Avery backtracked and said, "No, of course not. It's the fact that I overheard Willow ask Liam to train Bora, and considering both of your pasts, I don't think you would want to get involved."

"I'll talk to Liam, and we will work out an agreement for teaching Bora. We may have a messy past, but we are going to have to work together to get along. I'll talk to him during the night market."

"What's the night market?" I asked.

Nessa answered, "It's like the market in Bateau except it is on Saturday nights during the summer to avoid the heat."

"The whole town will be there. There will be food, music, and dancing," Avery said.

That was when a plan started to form in my head. I would attend the festival with the others, and afterward, I would leave that night without their knowledge. Over the next week, I acted normal while secretly packing things I would be needing while on my own. I went to Nessa's early one morning and asked her if she knew where my staff was. I told her I was feeling well enough and that I could start training again with it.

She reached under her bed and pulled it out and said, "I am glad you are feeling better, but don't overdo it."

On the day of the market, Nessa stopped by and gave me a wooden cat mask that was painted white. "There is no sense in advertising your presence here. The mask will help hide your identity. They actually sell them at the market, so you won't be the only one in a mask," she said.

I wore a plain blue dress and black flats, and my short hair hung down to help conceal my face. We all met up at the trailhead in the early evening before walking to the market. When we got close, I put my cat mask on. Kat was so fascinated with it, I ended up handing her over to Nessa to keep her from pulling off my mask.

The market glowed from all the lanterns that were hung by the booths. There were rows after rows of booths that seemed almost endless. In the middle of the market was a section for food and dancing. As we walked through the market, a booth in particular caught my attention. The booth was full of wooden masks. They came in a variety of painted faces, some human, some animal, and even some magical creatures. Avery picked up a fox mask that was actually only a half mask and handed the same one to Amos.

"Amos, we have to get these," she said.

"Why not?" Amos said as he handed a couple of coins to the booth attendant.

I looked around us and realized the rest of the group had already gone on ahead. "Ok, we need to get going now to catch up with the others," I said.

Avery and Amos both had their fox masks on. Avery hooked her arm on mine, and Amos on the other side of me hooked his arm around my other arm.

"You're both crazy," I said. *Oh, how I am going to miss them*, I thought to myself.

"What are you smiling at?" Avery questioned.

"Oh, I just didn't realize how much I could miss all of you," I said.

"Yeah, we missed you, too," Avery said.

"When you were in the coma, I had to keep telling everyone that you were going to be ok!" Amos said.

"I recall you harassing Willow on a daily basis. That's how worried you were."

Avery snapped and continued, "At least I didn't get kicked out of her room because I wouldn't leave her bedside."

Amos gave Avery an angry look and said, "That's not true."

"Yes, it is, Amos. You don't have to be embarrassed."

Amos then mouthed, "Please stop."

Avery, Amos, and I continued walking through the market until we reached the center. Avery quickly ran over and plopped herself down at an empty table.

"Avery, are you alright?" I asked.

"I am fine, just thirsty," she said.

Amos said, "I will get us a couple of drinks and walk away."

I watched as Amos got in line behind a pretty girl. She immediately turned and smiled at him and said something to him. Amos then laughed and took off the fox mask. They continued to smile and speak to each other. The girl inched closer to him and whispered something in his ear. Amos laughed so hard, we could hear it from where we were sitting. A few minutes later, Amos was back with our drinks. I noticed the girl did not take her eyes off of him.

She was looking me up and down, and I suddenly felt very silly in my cat mask.

"I hope you don't mind but I have been asked to dance and I felt like I couldn't say no," he said.

"That is fine," I said. "I hope you enjoy yourself."

After he walked away, Avery looked at me and said, "That did not sound very convincing."

I did not reply. I continued to watch Amos and the girl dance and smile at each other.

Avery then said, "This has been happening a lot lately to Amos. He seems to be getting a lot of attention from females lately. I think it has something to do with all that firewood he is always chopping."

This was the first time in my life that I had experienced jealousy, and I did not like it. After the music ended, Amos and the girl walked off the dance floor, and they stood to the side smiling and talking. He eventually looked back toward us, and I pretended not to notice him.

"Are you feeling alright? You don't seem to be yourself," Avery said.

"I am fine," I said. "Just tired."

Avery hugged me and said, "I am glad that you are alright. The rest will figure itself out."

Shortly after, Amos appeared and sat next to me. "Bora, would you like to dance?"

"No," I said. "I don't feel like dancing."

We sat and observed all the people who seemed to be having the time of their lives as we just sat there.

A thick layer of smells clung in the air from all the different foods that were being served. The music was loud, and there were young men dancing with beautiful women. Kyra was there dancing with several different men as well. Across the way, I was able to see Nessa bouncing Kat on her lap and talking to Willow.

Amos noticed me looking around and said, "Can I get you anything? "

"No, thank you," I said in a voice that was louder than my normal voice.

At that, Amos looked hurt. Amos then stood up and said, "I am going to go get something to eat," before he disappeared out of sight.

Avery then stood up and said, "I am hungry," before she also disappeared.

A few minutes later, Theron appeared out of nowhere carrying a small unique dark green hexagon-shaped bottle in hand.

"How are you, Theron?" I asked.

"Terrible," he said. "Your friend, Nessa, has decided to make me her pet project. She is going to heal me from all my pain. I am no longer allowed to drink alcohol. She has made me a tincture made from white willow bark, devil's claw, turmeric, and ginger."

"Is it helping?" I asked.

"I am not sure," he said, "but I can tell you it tastes absolutely horrible. I am allowed only three drops at a time under my tongue for pain. I am willing to give it a try. What do I have to lose? Nessa also made me a suave to rub on my skin. She says that she may not be able to entirely heal me, but she can make it much better."

"Do you know what is in the suave Nessa made for you?" I asked.

Theron took a deep breath and said, "Let me think. I believe calendula oil, milk thistle, samambaia, and something else but I don't remember."

I started to laugh.

Theron asked, "What is so funny?"

"I am sorry. I am not laughing at you. You just made me so very happy," I said.

"What are you doing here by yourself?" he said. "Shouldn't you be with the other two right now?"

I hesitated before replying, "I'm not hungry, so I stayed while the others went to go get something to eat."

Theron said bluntly, "That's a lie and we both know it. You're worried and scared."

I swallowed the lump in my throat before saying, "I am confused. I keep thinking I need to do something, but I don't know what it is and I am worried and scared about what will happen if I fail. What happens if Maverick finds out about me and I'll be public enemy number one? If I stay here with the people who care about me, I am putting all of them in danger."

"Not wrong," Theron said.

"I thought you came here to make me feel better?" I said.

"No matter what you do, people are going to get hurt even if it is unintentional. Don't worry so much; things always work out in the end," he said.

"For whom?" I asked. "For my mother and father, did things work out for them?"

"I am sorry, Bora," he said. "I don't have any answers for you, but you have people around you who care about you and are willing to fight to keep you safe."

"What can you tell me about Hewa? It was one of your territories?" I asked.

"No way in hell are you going there," he said. "Do you know how dangerous it is? How many women there go missing? You can't be serious. I forbid you to go there!"

"I was just asking. I thought maybe I could lie low there since it is so overcrowded," I said.

"Well, that is not going to happen," he said.

Theron's eyes then shot up behind me and he said, "This conversation isn't over!"

Then he stood up and walked away at a very fast pace. It didn't take me long to figure out what made Theron leave so quickly. Willow was making her way over to us. As she walked over, she was looking around.

She got closer and she asked, "Have you seen Theron? I just wanted to check in on him."

"He was just here complaining about the tincture Nessa gave him. Apparently, it tastes terrible. I am shocked he is willing to give it a try though. So don't push him too hard, or he will just go back to drinking," I said.

Willow asked, "Why are you sitting over here all by yourself?"

I looked around and saw Amos speaking to the girl who he had danced with earlier. Willow said, while gesturing to the two of them, "Are you ok with that?"

"I honestly don't care. I am happy that he has found someone," I said.

Willow looked at me, skeptical, and said, "Are you sure?"

"Yeah, why wouldn't I?" I said.

That was when Nessa came over and said, "Can you look after Kat while I stretch my legs?"

I nodded and held out my arms ready to accept Kat. When she placed Kat in my arms, she nuzzled into me and started to drift off to sleep.

"Traitor," Avery mumbled under her breath, as she sat down next to me.

Amos then came walking over and asked, "Are you sure I can't get you something to eat?"

"I told you I wasn't hungry," I said.

Amos gave me a serious look and said, "You haven't eaten since lunch; you need to eat," he said.

"Ok. Good point," I said.

Then Amos went off to get me something to eat. He was back in a few minutes with a plate filled with bread, meats, cheese, and olives. He handed it to me.

"It's perfect," I said. "Thank you."

Nessa, Avery, Amos all sat down with me still holding Kat. We all began to dig in. Nessa had a pea soup; Amos, a turkey leg bigger than his head. Kat had woken up; she and Avery were eating some shredded chicken and blueberries.

As we ate, Avery asked, "I saw you talking to Theron after we left. What did you talk about?"

At that, Nessa looked away and slurped her soup.

"Nessa had put Theron on a tincture for pain. I think he just wanted me to know he is trying," I said.

Nessa continued to avoid all of our eyes, and apparently, her ears had also failed.

"Really, Nessa, that is wonderful," Avery said.

Nessa just kept eating her pea soup and ignored Avery.

"Nessa," Avery said.

Nessa finally looked up and said, "Theron has a long way to go. There is no cause for celebration now."

I then turned to Amos and said, "Amos, who was that woman you were dancing with?"

"Her name is Claire. I have seen her around town before. She even bought some firewood from me. She has asked to dance with me again after we eat unless anyone has any objections?"

Everyone at the table looked at me. I could feel their eyes on me, but I refused to look up or even acknowledge what Amos had said.

The night continued. I felt grateful for being surrounded by my makeshift family. Around ten, we all headed back to our cabins and said our good nights. I finished getting everything ready to leave and waited until midnight. When I was sure everyone would be asleep, I crept out the cabin door.

After taking a few steps, I heard a gruff voice say, "Where are you going?"

I jumped and turned around. Then a bright light appeared. My eye shut tight before it eventually adjusted to the light. Nessa, Theron, and a tired-looking Willow were standing in front of me. Avery was leaning against a tree with Kat sleeping in her arms. Amos and Kyra were nowhere to be seen.

Theron then spoke again and stated, "I'll say it one more time. Where do you think you're going?"

I stood frozen and mumbled, "Hewa."

Avery chimed in and asked, "And why are you going there?"

"Because it's a good place to lie low," I said.

"Hewa is dangerous. Why would you go alone?" Avery said.

I spoke up and said, "You know how much I care about all of you. I am putting all of you in danger, and if you stay with me, then you may get hurt because of me."

Avery looked at me with pity.

Then Nessa said, "That's not what family is about. Family is having someone in your corner through thick and thin. So deal with it, because you're not getting rid of any of us that easily."

"You're all crazy," I chuckled.

Avery and Nessa replied at the same time, "Yes, we are."

Theron then spoke up and said, "Bora, you need to stay here for a few more days. We have some plans in motion. You will be leaving, but you won't be leaving alone. Some from the group will be leaving with you, and some of the group will stay here with Willow. She will watch over them and keep them safe. You need to trust us and know that your safety and the safety of your friends are our top priority."

"How many days are we talking about?" I asked.

"Less than a week," Theron added. "Can we get your word that you won't be

sneaking out again in the middle of the night, or do we need to have Amos sleep outside your cabin door?"

"That won't be necessary. You have my word. Thank you; thank you, everyone, for your help," I said. "Where is Amos anyway?" I asked.

Avery spoke up and said, "The last time I saw him, he was sleeping in a chair."

"Goodnight, Bora," Nessa said.

"Goodnight," Avery said.

Theron said, "See you in the morning."

CHAPTER 15

The Long Goodbye

THREE DAYS LATER, AN OLD woman showed up. Willow had told me to come see her the day before and told me to go to her cabin after breakfast. When I arrived at the cabin, the door was open, so I let myself in. Willow was sitting at her desk looking over a paper. Next to her was an odd-looking woman who seemed disinterested in whatever Willow was looking at.

"Good to see you here. Please close the door and have a seat. I am just going to finish looking over this," Willow said.

The woman next to Willow said, "It's right, so can we get started already. I don't have all day."

Willow replied, "Patience, Edith. I am almost done." Once Willow was done reading, she handed the paper over to Edith and said, "Bora, do you know why I called you here?"

I shook my head as Willow continued saying, "Today is the day you will be getting your eye back hopefully. Edith is here and is willing to assist us with putting it back where it rightfully belongs."

Edith said, "Sit down, girl, and take off your eyepatch so we can get started."

I did what she asked and took off the eyepatch. She then placed her hand over my empty eye socket.

"I am going to be awakening the nerves in your eye. You might feel some pain and pressure." Edith started to chant, "As do chodladh, as do chodladh, as do chodladh , as do chodladh."

Suddenly I felt as if I was being poked in my eye socket. She then quickly stopped. Willow then handed her the adder stone, and Edith started chanting again, "As do chodladh. as do chodladh, as do chodladh, as do chodladh,"

All the while Edith was rubbing and turning the adder stone over and over again in her hands. The adder stone started to glow brighter and brighter, and then a loud crack could be heard. Edith's hands were back in front of my face again. This time I felt a burning pain and almost passed out.

Then Edith said, "It is finished."

I then opened my eye slowly, but all I could see was black.

"Give it a minute, dear," Edith said.

The black turned slowly to gray and then suddenly to white. Then colors came into view. A vase filled with flowers was sitting on the desk.

I covered my other eye with my hand and yelled out, "I can see! Oh thank you, Edith, you did it. I can see."

Edith then said, "Congratulations, your eye is back. I would like my pay now," and held out one of her hands.

Willow said, "Why must you ruin this sweet moment?" while placing a bag of coins in her hand.

"Pleasure doing business with you," Edith said, while walking to the door.

"Wait. You're not going to tell anyone about this?" I asked.

Edith turned around and said, "No, it is really no one's business. I wouldn't be in business long if I divulged secrets."

"Edith, we appreciate your help. I put a little extra in the pouch for you," Willow said.

Before she left I yelled, "Thank you, Edith!"

Then she was gone without another word. I ran to the bathroom and stared at myself in the mirror. I was back to being my old self again. I ran out of the bathroom and hugged Willow.

"Thank you, Willow, for doing this for me," I said.

"I am glad to help you, Bora. You look wonderful."

"I can't wait to show Avery and Amos and Nessa."

I said thank you again as I ran out of the door. I found Nessa and Kat first out by the garden. Nessa hugged me.

"I am so happy for you," she said.

After that, I went off in search of Avery and Amos. I found them on the trailhead leading into Bartrex. Amos was pulling a wagon filled with firewood, while Avery was pushing from behind.

"Hey," I yelled, "wait up."

I ran to them out of breath, unable to speak.

Avery made an ugly face and said, "Bora, we talked about this. You can't come with us to Bartrex. It may not be safe for you."

I stood there in disbelief.

Then Amos said, "You got your eye back. You look beautiful."

Avery screamed, "No way! How did this happen?"

"Willow found a witch who was able to reverse the spell. Theron had gone back to the river the next day after he rescued me and found the adder stone."

Avery then gave me a hug.

Amos said, "Congratulations, Bora, but you really need to go back so you aren't seen on this trailhead. Tonight we will celebrate."

"Ok," I said. "See you tonight."

That night, at dinner, everyone was together. Even Theron was in a festive mood considering he still was not drinking. Liam had arrived earlier that day, and he and Kyra were even pleasant to each other. After dinner, Liam stood up and said that he had an announcement to make.

"First, I want to congratulate Bora on getting her eye back. Second, Bora, Theron, Krya, and I will be leaving tomorrow."

"Where are we going?" I asked.

"Bora, we will be taking you to a deserted island for training. We are going to work on getting you to transform. You will be in no position to take on Maverick if you are unable to transform," he said.

"I understand," I said.

"I believe Nessa also has some news she would like to share," Liam said.

Liam then sat down and Nessa Stood up.

"I have some wonderful news to share."

Nessa continued, "Avery, Amos, Kat, and I will also be leaving very soon. We have pulled together all our money and bought a small farm on the outskirts of Hewa. After you mentioned going to Hewa, Bora, that put an idea in our heads. Since Hewa is one of Maverick's territories and he never goes there, it is probably the safest place for us to be. The farm we bought is eighteen miles from Hewa, so we will be able to sell the food we grow and I will be able to sell my medicines. Bora, when you are done with your training, we will be waiting for you to join us."

I couldn't believe my ears. It all sounded so wonderful. We all will be together, and we will be safe. Maverick won't be looking for a ghost. That night, I could not sleep. After tossing and turning for hours, I decided to take a walk. The moon was partially hidden by large dark clouds. After only a few minutes, a shadow appeared in front of me.

Then a voice spoke, "You can't sleep either."

"Amos, is that you?" I asked.

"Yes, it's me," he said, and he took a step and he was standing directly in front of me. "Tomorrow is a big day for you," he said.

"Yeah," I said and continued, "It might be a while before we are all together again."

He did not answer, and the next thing I knew, I could feel his lips on mine. I did not move away, and I kissed him back hard and my arms wrapped around his wide large shoulders.

After a few minutes, he pulled away and said, "I am going to miss you. You better go get some sleep. Tomorrow will be a long day for you."

I kissed him again quickly and walked away back to my little cabin. I did not get any sleep that night. The kiss with Amos kept playing in my head, and I was no longer excited about leaving the next day.

The next morning, it was time to leave. I headed to the hidden meadow where we all agreed to meet. Liam and Theron were standing there waiting for everyone to arrive.

"Are you ready to go?" Theron asked.

"Yeah, I am ready," I said.

Willow and Nessa came walking up with Kat in Nessa's arms.

"Let me say goodbye before you go," Nessa said. I then hugged Nessa, and she said, "Take care of yourself."

"I will," I said.

Kat was in her arms, and she was reaching up trying to grab me. I held her tight and kissed her on the forehead before handing her back to Nessa.

Next, Willow gave me a hug and said, "We will meet again, my dear."

"Thank you for everything, Willow. You didn't have to take us all in, but you did. We are all indebted to you."

Amos then came over and kissed me on the lips. He then turned around and walked away without saying a word. Avery had a surprised look on her face as she hugged me.

She then said, "I am going to miss you."

I held her tightly and said, "I am going to miss you, too."

After a few seconds, Theron said, "Break it up, ladies. We need to go."

Avery and I pulled apart, and Liam said, "We are still waiting for Kyra."

After a few minutes, Kyra came running toward us with her bag in hand. Kyra said, "Sorry I'm late. Lost track of time."

Liam said, "You're looking well. With you here now, we can discuss who is going to carry Bora."

"I can carry her," Kyra said.

"Perfect. That means Liam can carry me," Theron said.

"You are perfectly capable of flying all by yourself. Why should I carry you?"

Theron replied, "We don't want to draw any extra unwanted attention to us. It's not often that you see more than two dragons flying together."

"Good point," Liam said. "Let's go."

After a few days of travel, we arrived on the island where they would begin to work with me. We lived in a cave on the deserted island to remain hidden so no one would see us. At nighttime, we built a fire to keep us warm. The girls slept on the right side of the cave, while the boys slept on the left. During the day, when we weren't training, we were catching fish and boiling water to drink. Liam had brought some supplies prior to our arrival since the island was short on all supplies except for fresh fish and coconuts. Theron's mood worsened toward all of us to the point where every other thing he said was a complaint.

Near the island, there was a reef where the mermaids liked to hang out. The female mermaids were extremely attentive toward Liam and Theron and treated Kyra and I with contempt. Liam refused to go into the water or use his water powers because the mermaids wouldn't keep their hands off of him. They would circle him constantly while he was in the water, touching him and making clicking sounds. I had never seen a mermaid before, only pictures in a book or carved images on the bow of a ship. They were strange-looking creatures; their faces were very thin, and their mouths were extremely wide. The shape of their face was more like a fish than of a human.

Kyra refused to fish; she said gathering food was a man's job. The problem was Kyra also refused to cook or even boil drinking water. Liam did his best to ignore the mermaids, while Theron seemed to enjoy the attention. The mermaids made fishing a lot easier by throwing fish at us while we stood on the shore holding our fishing poles. The fish would land at the feet of Liam and Theron. As for me, they would cackle and cheer every time they threw a fish and it hit me. At first, it really bothered me, but I soon came to appreciate the free meal. I would pretend that I was mad when I was hit with a fish and sometimes pretended the fish hitting me would hurt. This would encourage them to throw more fish at me. Every day, I would catch at least twice as much fish as compared to Liam and Theron.

My transformation training was not going so well. I did however start to feel much stronger. That night after dinner, Liam mentioned that Nessa, Kat, Avery, and Amos would be leaving the next day for their new farm. Theron had helped them make all the arrangements; he even found the farm for them and worked as a middleman to secure the property. He described it as a small farm with thirty-five acres of land. It had a small blue house with three bedrooms and a red barn that was slightly bigger than the home. The barn was stocked with goats, chickens, and a few cows. The seed for the next planting season had already been purchased and came with the property. Liam said it would be a four-day walk for them to reach the farm, but they were in for a big surprise.

"What big surprise?" I asked.

"They would not be walking because Theron and Willow have purchased one of the largest horses any of them had ever seen and an equally large wagon, because every farm needs a good plow horse."

"What? No," I said. "You all have been so generous. Thank you, Theron, and thank you, Liam and Kyra. I don't know how I will ever repay all of you."

I lay in bed that night imagining the morning sun rising and the group wanting to get an early start. The group would be so excited to finally be heading home. It had been so long since any of them had a home to call their own. They would say their goodbyes to Willow who would be waiting for them. Then Willow would surprise them with a new horse and wagon. Nessa, Avery, Amos, and Kat would all thank her and hug Willow and say their goodbyes. Amos would help the women and Kat up into the wagon, and they would be on their way.

Every day, Kyra and I sparred on the sandbank during low tide. She eventually started to throw insults at me, trying to make me angry. Liam had said that it was easier to transform while being angry.

Kyra had taken that to heart and started verbally insulting me. Kyra and I sparred while she used a sword while I used my scythe. Any time she would swing her sword, I would block her strike. After more than a couple of days without any sign of transformation, everyone was getting frustrated.

At first, Kyra would say, "Come on; you can do better than that." Then she would call me "weak and pathetic." At first, I thought it was amusing, but then she said, "I hope you know Amos is going to get bored of you in no time at all and he will leave you."

After that, I had had enough and started throwing insults back. I replied, "That's rich coming from you. No wonder Liam never asked you to marry him. You on the other hand are only focused on making Liam jealous. So how pathetic are you?"

Once I said that, Kyra lowered her sword and walked away without saying another word to me for two days. After that, Liam became my sparring partner. He was so much stronger and faster than Kyra was, and I struggled blocking his hits. Afterward, he told me that he was holding back because he did not want to hurt me.

That night at dinner, we ate hogfish. Kyra still was not talking to me. We were all so miserable, and it showed. Theron was still taking the tincture that Nessa had given him. It had become apparent that Theron was struggling with withdrawals. I was feeling terrible. I felt responsible for everyone's unhappiness.

"Liam, thank you for cooking the fish," I said.

"No problem. It would be better if some people pulled their weight, but alas that is too much to ask for from some people," Liam said.

Theron said, "If you ask me, that fish was way undercooked."

"Theron, how is your side?" I asked.

Theron pulled up the side of his shirt showing his blackened skin that seemed to have gotten worse. Liam looked away as Kyra started to gag from looking at it.

Theron then said, "It's horrible! I have never been so miserable."

"Theron, I know you're in pain, but Nessa is trying to help you," I said.

"Help?" Theron yelled. "Does this look like help to you?" Theron then threw his coconut and it hit the cave wall and smashed into pieces, and he said, "I have had this curse longer than all of you have been alive. I know how to manage it. All people ever do is make things worse."

"Theron, please calm down," I said.

"How can a naive girl like you ever become queen? Clearly saving you was more than I bargained for. Liam is unwilling to really fight with you and only training you because, in the slim chance that you do become queen, he can keep his high status. Kyra only tagged along because she doesn't trust you with Liam, being the envious woman she is. So, Bora, tell me what you think of us now that you know our true intentions?"

I looked around at Liam and Kyra. Neither of them was willing to meet my eyes.

I then stood up and said, "Liam, I would like to leave now. Considering how much of a bother I am to you all, it would be better if I just left."

"You're not a bother, but I think you're right: we should all go. We aren't accomplishing anything except making each other miserable. Go get your stuff. We can leave right away. I won't miss sleeping on the cave floor tonight." Liam stretched and asked, "Where am I taking you?"

"The farm near Hewa where the others are. You will be dropping me off there."

Theron said, "I think you should stay and continue to work on your transformation."

"I am done, Theron. It's obvious that I am unable to transform. I am good with that. You can't make me into something I am not," I said.

Then I turned around and walked away to the cave exit. Kyra followed after me trying to talk to me, but I just ignored her.

Once I was out of the cave, Kyra said, "Bora, come on talk to me. At least say one word."

I said, "How about two words? Go away."

She then grabbed my upper arm forcing me to look at her and said, "Please let's talk this out."

I pulled my arm out of her grip and said, "You and the others were just using me for your own benefit. I can't trust that you have my best interests in mind anymore."

Kyra did not say anything and instead let me go. Liam then came out of the cave and shifted into his dragon form. I climbed on Liam and looked at Kyra and Theron. Kyra had her arm crossed over her chest looking sad.

Theron was smoking a cigar, and without looking at me, he said, "Hurry up and go already, but you should know that before we left to come to this island, I had gotten word that Maverick had ordered every tracker of the kingdom to search the river and even out into the sea for your dead body. He is even offering a high reward to whoever finds your body. So keep your head down and stay out of Hewa. The second you leave, I will be leaving and going back to Arm."

"What about me?" Kyra said.

"What about you?" Theron said.

Kyra replied, "Where am I supposed to go?"

Theron said, "I don't care where you go as long as it is away from me."

As Theron and Kyra continued to bicker, Liam took off escaping the argument and flying away.

After two days, in the early morning, we finally reached the farmlands outside of Hewa. I kept an eye out for a small blue farmhouse that Nessa had described to me as our new home. In the distance, I could see the blue little house with smoke coming out of the chimney. I imagined them all sitting and eating breakfast together, my family of misfits. Liam saw the little blue house too and went down to land in a nearby field. Within minutes, we were on the ground. He quickly transformed into his human self.

"Will you be coming to see the others with me? " I asked.

"No. I will say my goodbye to you here, Bora. This didn't turn out the way we all had hoped, and I am truly sorry for that," he said.

"If you or the others ever need anything, please find a way to let me know. I wish you the best of luck, and I wish you peace and happiness in your new life. Remember to keep your head down; danger lurks around every corner."

I hugged Liam.

"Thank you for everything," I said. "When you see Theron and Kyra, tell them thank you from me and that I am sorry that I was such a disappointment to them."

Liam shook his head. "You are not a disappointment to anyone. Now go and be happy."

I turned and looked at the little blue house and turned back to Liam just as he was taking off.

"Thank you," I yelled.

The door opened on the little blue house, and Nessa stood there holding Kat on her hip. Nessa yelled, "Bora's here. Bora's home."

Home—I was home with people who loved and cared about me. I walked up the path to the little blue house, and Ryder was sitting on the front porch.

As I entered the house, I said, "Good morning, Dad. It's great to be home."